THE *Jackpot* SCREWER   1

THE Jackpot SCREWER

LOVE IN *Dayton Valley* SERIES BOOK 2

NIKKI ASHTON

THE *Jackpot* SCREWER

WARNING

This book contains scenes of a sexy man being kind to
children and puppies
Please don't read standing up in case you swoon

THE *Jackpot* SCREWER

DEDICATION

This book is for my gorgeous niece, Peggy Casewell
Never stop being independent and brave.

ACKNOWLEDGMENTS

Wow, what a joy it has been writing this the second book in the Dayton Valley series. I had no idea when I started how much I would grow to love these characters. Therefore, my first thanks go to the Maples, Jackson and Delaney families for talking to me and pretty much creating yourselves. I only hope you the reader love them and their craziness as much as I do.

Obviously, this book isn't all down to me. I write the words and rely on a whole host of other people to get it out to you, the reader. So, here come the thank yous.

My alpha team - Donna, Lynn and Sarah. Without them and their guidance on plotlines and keeping me on the straight and narrow you could well be getting a murder mystery set on a pig farm in Norfolk—nothing wrong with that but not what I promised to write.

My beta readers, Cal, Sophie, Kimberley and Leanne who were the first to read the finished book and luckily loved it. A note to everyone—Carter belongs to Sophie and she will fight you for him if the need arises!

Anna Bloom for her usual work of excellence in the editing department. You have no idea how many times you could have been reading the words real and evidently but for her.

Lou Stock for the absolutely gorgeous cover. It is Bronte to a T. Also, thank you Lou for finding me the star who is Flora Burgos. Thank you, Flora, for getting my Texan right and being so sweet and kind.

I have to mention my Carter muse—I have no idea why I do this because they never see it. However, thank you to the gorgeous redhead, Ken Beck. You sir are a vision to behold and you can certainly stroke my puppies any day of the week.

Mr. A also gets a mention. His encouragement and love are sometimes what keep me going. The days when things are getting a little dark in the book world, he reminds me why I write—because I love making people smile. His words and the offer to pour me a rum and coke usually get me focused again.

As usual I want to thank you the reader. You may not always read the acknowledgements, but you really should. Be assured almost every writer will thank you because we couldn't do this without you. Writing is hard work and lonely at times and we don't always please everyone, no matter how hard we try. We are human and will make mistakes. We are emotional and get upset when people don't like our words. We are however appreciative of every one of you for taking the time to read our books. So, thank you and here's to a better future for all of us.

CHAPTER 1

Carter

"Lollipop, open the damn door."

"Go away, you pickle stealer."

I swung around to face my best friend. "What the hell is she talking about? Why is she going on about me stealing some damn non-existent pickle?"

Hunter shrugged but had a huge, teeth flashing grin on his face, which was totally unwarranted. We were outside my girlfriend's house because only an hour ago she ended our relationship. In the local bar of all places. I had no idea why, only that she'd accused me of being a pickle stealer and said we were over – *she doesn't even eat pickles!*

What made it worse was that it had all happened in front of my sister and best friend, who'd recently started going out. They were sickeningly loved up and had just returned from a quick sex session. Where they'd had sex, who the hell knew, but while they both had satisfied and smug grins, I was shrouded in misery and trying to reason with Bronte.

"This is not funny, dick head," I hissed at Hunter. "If my sister ended things with you because you'd stolen her invisible pickle, I doubt you'd be smiling like that."

"One, I would never steal Ellie's pickle, and two, what the fuck? *Lollipop?*"

"And?" I asked, frowning at him. "You don't have a cute nickname for Ellie?"

He colored a little and moved to bang on the Jackson's door. "Bronte, just come out and speak to him."

"What is it?" I asked giving him a wink, my misery momentarily forgotten as I tried to work out what nickname he could have for my sister. "Tell me, I won't repeat it."

Hunter rolled his eyes. "Yeah right. It's marginal who's the biggest gossip in this town you or Mrs. Callahan at the gas station. Anyway, *if* I have a nickname for Ellie, and that's a big if, it'd between me and her."

At that moment, my sister walked out of the house. She looked a little mystified and was shaking her head. "She won't come out and she won't tell me what you did."

"I didn't do anything," I protested. "Not a damn thing. I even told her how good her tits were looking."

"Well, that's a little bit caveman and not the most romantic of compliments." Ellie sighed. "But even for Bronte, it's a little harsh to dump you on your ass for praising her assets."

"Exactly." I threw my hands into the air. "She's definitely hormonal, like I said."

Ellie's eyes hardened as she widened her stance. "You did not?"

"Yeah, she was being bitchy, so I said I didn't realize it was *that* time of the month."

Hunter winced. "Shit man, that was totally the wrong thing to say."

"No wonder she dumped you." Ellie glared at me before turning to Hunter. "Let's go. I can't deal with his stupidity any longer, plus remember Dad took Mom away for the weekend, so we have the house to ourselves."

My best friend grinned like he was the fox who'd stolen the fattest chicken from the coop. "Okay, let's go."

"So, you're not going to help me?" I asked as they both turned and practically ran for Hunter's truck.

"Sorry, but your sister needs my full attention." He took Ellie's hand and brought it to his mouth, kissing the back of it.

"You disgust me," I called. "You know that?"

Hunter flipped me off over his shoulder without even looking back.

"Hey, Ellie," I shouted.

"What?" she asked with a sigh, pulling up short and turning toward me.

"What's Hunt's cute little nickname for you?"

She shrugged her shoulders and answered, "Cutie pie, why?" at the same time as Hunter shouted, "Don't tell him."

"Why'd you tell him?" Hunter asked as he dragged her away.

"He asked." Ellie sounded a little frustrated.

"Yeah, well now he's going to give me shit about it."

"But I am your cutie pie."

I rolled my eyes as my sister pushed up on her toes and kissed the life out of my best friend.

"Please, just go," I called to them. "Leave me to my damn misery."

Laughing and tangled in each other, they stumbled to Hunter's truck. When it finally rumbled away down the quiet street where the Bronte and her family lived, I turned back to the door. It felt impenetrable, like the drawbridge of some damn castle I couldn't scale up to reach the damsel.

However, I was never one to quit. Fisting my hand, I banged on it again.

"Bronte. Open up or I swear I'll stay here all night. Maybe I'll even start singing."

We Maples were not the best of singers, and Bronte had often likened mine to the sound of a mule with a head cold.

"I mean it," I cried. "I can sing the whole Blur back catalog if you want me to."

British Indie bands were *our* thing and Bronte particularly liked Blur. I knew it would hurt her feelings if I ruined her favorite tune.

"I could murder Tender right here, right now, if you want me to."

Within seconds the door swung open and Bronte stood in front of me looking as damn beautiful as ever, with her blue and purple hair hanging in beach-waved tendrils around her face and over her amazing bigger-than-usual tits.

"Don't you dare," she hissed as she rubbed at her nose with a handkerchief and then swiped away a stray tear.

I took a step closer and held my hand out to her. "Lollipop baby, please tell me what I've done wrong. How can I fix it, if you don't tell me?"

"You can't fix it," she yelled, stamping her foot. "Nothing can fix it. Things will never be the same again."

I took a deep breath and tried not to show my frustration. We'd only been together a few months, but I'd known Bronte all her life. That meant I knew exactly when to let her know she pissed me off and when not to – the when was usually when she was horny because I knew my being all macho and angry got me some extra action in the bedroom. The when not, well that was times like now when she was obviously upset about something, even if I had no idea what it was, or why the fuck I was suddenly a pickle stealer.

I took a breath to beat down any sharpness in my tone and took her hand in mine. "Please, Lollipop, tell me what's wrong."

She took a deep breath and watched me carefully, her chin quivering as she contemplated whether I was worthy of an explanation.

"Well?" I coaxed.

"I'm pregnant," she blurted out. "You impregnated me, you stupid idiot. You and your super swimmers made a baby."

The last thing I remember was the image of Bronte going all fuzzy and me shouting out, "It's a lie." .

CHAPTER 2

Bronte

C arter sipped the sweet tea and eyed me warily, like it was all my fault.

Okay, I was fifty percent culpable, but he'd been the one to put his dick inside of me. And okay, so I'd asked him to, but how was I to know that the one time we forgot to use a condom he'd manage to hit the jackpot.

"Well." I sighed crossing my arms over my already sensitive boobs. "It's pretty obvious that you're not happy about the situation. I mean, unless of course you're having sympathetic fainting spells. Just wait until the labor pains."

The impregnator's face blanched and he took another huge gulp of tea.

"Nothing to say?" I snapped. "Okay, well I guess we're done here."

"No," Carter cried and put his cup down. "I have plenty to say. Like, how?"

"Well, I don't know if you remember," I replied with a bite. "But you put your penis inside my vagina and wiggled about a bit and then collapsed on top of me and began snoring in my ear."

"That was not how it went," Carter cried. "And you know it."

He was right, I did know it. It was *so* much better than that, but I'd be damned if I'd let him know. After all, he'd given me a baby which I wasn't ready for.

"You and me," Carter said, getting up from the sofa. "We are dynamite in bed, especially as I always put one hundred percent into everything I do."

"Yeah, you do," I snarked. "And this time you not only put one hundred percent in but a damn baby too."

Not wanting him to see me cry again, I turned away and took a deep breath. This could not be happening to me. It was the worst possible time. I was twenty-four years old and was only a year into owning my beauty salon. I loved going out and getting drunk with Ellie or fooling around with Carter, I wasn't ready to be a mother. Shit, my own family was falling apart, how the hell could I create another with the idiot standing opposite to me. There was no way he was ready.

"You can't even do your own laundry," I burst out. "How the hell are you supposed to bring up a child?"

If I'd expected Carter to give me any assurances, I'd have been wrong. He simply shrugged and fell weakly back onto the sofa.

I'd known this would be his reaction. Deep down, I'd guessed he'd be real unhappy about it. God knew I wasn't actually ecstatic about it myself. That's why I'd ended things with him. Maybe it had been a spur of the moment decision. A whim based on his stupid face when he'd asked me what was wrong, but it was the right decision all the same.

"I think you should go," I said moving toward the door. "Mom will be home soon, and I need to tell her."

Carter nodded slowly and stood up again. "Don't you think we should tell her together? Or maybe I should come with you to see your dad."

My parents were currently 'taking some time out' and Dad was renting an apartment in the same block as Carter, on the other side of town. They'd been having therapy for the last four weeks since Dad moved out and Mom was hopeful. Apparently, Mom had felt neglected for the last year and Dad just didn't see why. He thought buying her new boobs was showing her plenty of attention; Mom thought it meant he didn't like her old ones. And they say the parents are the sensible ones.

"I'll tell him myself," I replied. "I'll be doing this by myself anyway. I may as well start now."

Carter took a step back. "Who says you're doing it alone?"

"Well me." I shrugged. "It's obvious this isn't what you want, so…"

"Is it what you want?" he asked. "Is it what you planned for?"

"No, of course it wasn't what I planned for."

"But you're going to do it, anyway, be a mom?"

"Of course, I am."

His eyes went dark as he pushed his hands to his hips. "Well, then so am I. We are both responsible."

I wasn't sure he was being totally honest with himself and I couldn't afford to be taken halfway down a road, for him to suddenly stop and say, 'actually I wanna go back now'.

"I don't think you have any idea what this entails, Carter."

"Do you, Lollipop?" He looked at me earnestly, moving toward me. "Don't you think it's something we can figure out together?"

"Life would be so much easier, if I said yes," I replied, letting out a heavy sigh. "But this isn't what you want. You want to take over the veterinarian practice and carry on having boy's nights with Hunter whenever you can."

"Don't tell me what I want, Bronte," Carter said in a low tone. "You and I discussed moving in together, didn't we? I wouldn't have done that if I didn't want to. That shows you I'm committed to you."

I let out an empty laugh. "Moving in and having a baby together are two very different things. Just take the get out of jail free card, Carter. Once the baby is here if you still feel the same way, well then I'll let you be fully involved in its life."

His face screwed up into anger as he stalked to within inches of me. "Oh, you'll let me, will you? Gee that's real kind of you, Bronte."

"I'm giving you an opportunity," I cried. "To be single but be involved if you want to be."

"Maybe I don't want to be single." He gripped his hair and then turned to pace back toward the sofa.

His shoulders were hunched as he dragged a hand through his beautiful hair, the color of cinnamon sticks it was flecked with gold highlights when the sun shone on it. Through all the years we'd known each other and had fought and disliked each other, I never thought I'd end up loving him. I did though. I adored him and hated the idea of not being loved by him, or fighting with him, but this was something he was just not ready for and I didn't want my heart broken.

"Well I do," I finally replied. "I do want to be single. I want to do this alone."

Carter swung around to face me, his eyes as big as saucers. "Like hell you will."

"Can't stop me," I said defiantly. "Not unless you kidnap me and hold me hostage in your apartment."

"Yeah well," he cried, stamping a foot. "I may just do that."

"Like to see you try."

"Don't tempt me, Lollipop."

We weren't getting anywhere, and I knew that knowing us as I did, we could end up arguing until Hunter's rooster crowed. I wanted Carter gone before my mom and youngest brother, Austen, got home from visiting with my Aunt Willoughby – yeah, my mom got her love of the classics from Grandma who named both her daughters after Jane Austen *heroes* no less. And, for all I'd said about telling them, I actually wasn't ready to tell my parents, or anyone, about the baby.

"Listen," I said, knowing that I needed to placate Carter. "I think we both need to sleep on this. I'm not going to tell my folks yet, I'm only nine weeks, so anything could happen."

Carter's eyes went immediately to my belly where my hands rested. "You're being careful though?"

"Yes, Carter, I'm being careful." I pinched the bridge of my nose, suddenly feeling more tired than I ever remembered. "Let's just keep it between us for now."

"And what about us?" he asked, straightening to his full height and pulling back his shoulders.

I had to be honest with him, but I also had to think about what was to come. "You know how I feel about you, but it's not just me now. I need to think of the baby."

"And you don't think I will," he answered.

I shrugged. "We've been having fun and while it was going somewhere, me moving in may not be an option any longer. It won't just be me, so I need you to be sure that you're okay with that."

Carter silently contemplated what I'd said and then nodded. "Okay. You win, for now, but I'll prove to you this is something I'm committed to."

I breathed out a relieved sigh. "Good. That's all I want."

He watched me carefully and rubbed at his chin.

"What?"

"So, while we're taking things slow, do we still get to have sex? Because I've got to tell you Lollipop your tits look a-maz-ing."

And that, ladies and gentlemen, is why I worried that Carter Maples wasn't up to the job of being my baby daddy.

CHAPTER 3

Carter

Nursing my bottle of beer, I sighed heavily until Hunter punctuated it with a groan.

"What?" I snapped my head up and gave him the dead eye.

"I'm just sick of hearing you sighing instead of doing something about the fact she dumped you."

"There's nothing that can be done, dickhead."

"Well, if you damn well told me *why* she dumped you, I might be able to help."

The door to an almost empty Stars & Stripes swung open and Jacob Crowne walked in, looking even more downcast than I did. Hunter and I were sitting at the bar in easy view and Jacob gave us a chin lift as he walked over.

"Hey, guys."

Hunter and I replied in kind as Penny approached Jacob.

"Usual?"

Jacob nodded solemnly.

"Don't often see you in here on a Saturday afternoon, you're usually busy at the shop," she said as she pulled him a draft of beer.

"Yeah, well." His nostrils flared with a heavy breath. "Let's just say it's women problems."

Penny arched her brows and took the money that Jacob was offering to her.

"You should hook up with Carter," Hunter said. "He's got problems with his better half too."

"I can assure you, without wanting to sound like a douche, there is nothing *better* about my wife."

I winced. "That bad, huh?"

"Yep. That bad." Jacob then proceeded to gulp down more than half his drink. Finally, he slammed his glass down and wiped his mouth with the back of his hand. "Guess you may as well be the first in town to know, Lydia has pretty much moved out and we are no longer together."

"Shit," Hunter replied. "I'm so sorry, Jacob."

"Don't be. It's been a long time coming."

Penny patted Jacob's hand. "You want another, honey?"

He shook his head. "No, I was just giving her long enough to get the last of her shit out of my house. I need to collect JJ from his play date soon."

"The *last* of her shit?" I asked. "So, this has been coming a while."

"Christmas was kind of the breaking point. Don't want to go into too much detail, I have JJ to think of, but let's say she's not the woman, wife or mother, I thought she was. My son is my priority, so me and her are done. JJ is staying with me."

Hunter and I watched him silently as he drained the rest of his glass. He then got up, gave us another chin lift and left.

"Shit," I groaned. "Being an adult kind of stinks. I don't think I want to be one."

Hunter laughed. "Well, I'm pretty sure there's not much you can do about it."

Thinking of Bronte and the baby growing inside of her, I had to agree with him. I loved my life, it was carefree and fun, even working twelve-hour days like I regularly did never seemed much of a chore. As for me and Bronte, well we were just getting started and having a child was certainly going to change all that. While I loved her and wanted us to be together, no matter what, I also realized that our lives were going to change drastically. They were going to get a lot harder. That thought had my stomach roiling and set my nerves jangling.

"Bronte's pregnant," I blurted out.

Hunter dropped his bottle of beer with a thud on the bar and reared back. "Say what?"

"You heard me." I swallowed hard. "That's why she's pissed at me."

"You're having a baby," he hissed, chancing a glance at Penny who was cleaning down at the other end of the bar. "Are you fucking insane? Actually no, scratch that, is *she* fucking insane?"

I shrugged. "She's kind of insane *and* angry. In fact, I'm petrified of her because she's so damn angry. She actually hit me with her mom's broom when she threw me out last night for suggesting we still have sex even though we broke up."

"So, she let you in after we left?" Hunter asked.

"Yeah, well she kind of had to." I scratched at the scruff on my cheek and grimaced. "I passed out when she told me."

There was a moment, just a tiny moment, when I thought Hunt was being sympathetic and a good friend. That moment didn't last before he almost busted his guts by letting out a huge roar of laughter.

"Not funny, man." I punched him in his shoulder, but he was too busy laughing to notice. "I mean it, shut the fuck up."

"You fainted. Wait until I tell Ellie, she'll piss her pants."

"No," I cried, grabbing hold of his arm. "You can't tell her. Bronte swore me to secrecy."

"I won't tell her why, just that you did." He slapped my back. "If you think I'm wasting that little fucking nugget you are so wrong my friend."

"Why the hell are you my best friend?" I threw my hands into the air. "Actually, you know what, you don't need to be any longer. I'll get someone else. I'll ask Alaska."

That made Hunter laugh even louder. "You can't interview for the job and when did you develop a stammer."

Frowning, I shrugged. "What the hell are you talking about?"

"You'll ask Alaska," he repeated, but I looked at him blankly. "Do you not realize how funny that is; you'll ask Alaska. *I'll ask her*, get it?"

"But he's a guy," I replied, frowning.

"Yeah, but it's still fucking funny," Hunter replied, almost doubled over laughing at his own shit joke.

I breathed out through my nose and wondered why everyone thought Hunter was the sensible one in our friendship. "I don't have the energy to tell you what an absolute dick you are. Just don't you dare tell Ellie about…" I looked around and then moved closer to whisper, "…the baby."

Rubbing at his chest, Hunter retrieved his bottle of beer and took a quick drink. "I don't have secrets from her," he announced.

"You've only been together like two months, of course you have secrets."

"Nine weeks and two days to be precise."

What the…

"You know exactly how long you've been together?" Damn I really was shit at the boyfriend thing. I could hazard a guess that Bronte and I had been together around five months—or so—but not the exact amount of time.

"What? You don't know when you started dating Bronte?" Hunter asked, a smug look on his face.

I shrugged. "It's difficult to say. We were just messing around to start with. I do know the first time we had sex was Karaoke night in here, on Minnesota's birthday."

Hunter scratched his head and frowned.

"Remember Bronte disappeared and texted Ellie to say she had a headache?"

"Yeah, vaguely."

"And then I had that emergency."

"Oh yeah, you left me having to watch Dominic the dick with his hands all over my woman."

I rolled my eyes. "Ellie wasn't your woman then. She wasn't even on your radar."

Hunter grinned and shook his head. "I think she's always been on my radar, but I was just too stupid to realize."

"Whatever. The point I'm making is she didn't have a headache and there was no emergency. I'd already kissed her outside the bathrooms, so we agreed I'd leave first and then she'd follow me ten minutes later."

Hunter looked shocked. "One kiss, after years of hating each other, caused you to hook up?"

"Judgy much, says you who did exactly the same with my sister."

"We had two kisses," Hunter growled with narrow eyes on me. "Belinda's party and then singles night. Admittedly the kiss on singles night was on the way to store closet where we had sex, but that's just splitting hairs." Ignoring him, I nodded to Penny for two more beers. "And it doesn't change the fact you don't know how long you've been with your girlfriend," he carried on, "which kind of explains why she dumped you."

I swung around on my stool to face him. "She dumped me because I impregnated her, and she thinks I don't want to be a dad and won't manage the responsibility."

Hunter's head tilted to one side as he examined me. "Do you? Will you?"

My pause must have said too much because Hunter groaned and scrubbed a hand down his face.

"You need to step up man," he said, glancing at Penny who was holding out two beers.

I took them both and handed one to Hunter and then waited for Penny to leave. When she moved back to the other end of the bar, I let out a sigh.

"It was a shock. We both need to get used to it, so swear you won't say anything to Ellie. Please, Hunt. I don't want my folks to know until Bronte and I have had a chance to get our heads sorted."

"Fuck, Carter, I hate lying to her."

"You won't be lying, just keeping a secret. Bronte will kill me if she knows I told you."

Finally, after a few seconds of watching me, Hunter nodded. "Fine, but if Ellie finds out I knew and didn't tell her, it'll be your balls I'll be using to replace the ones I lose."

Breathing out a sigh of relief, we lapsed into silence which was rudely broken by the door swinging open and landing hard against the wall. I half expected to see Jacob again, so I was surprised when in walked my sister and Bronte.

"Ah shit," Bronte cried as soon as she saw us. "As if my day couldn't get any shitter."

Ellie pulled up short and threw an anxious glance at Hunter.

"I thought you were going to the Mall," he said getting up and kissing her cheek.

"We were but Bronte decided she wanted some of Penny's pot pie instead." Ellie turned back to Bronte. "You want to go?"

My eyes drank Bronte in as she considered her options. Her hair was tied up in some weird bun things on each side of her head and her eye make-up was purple and blue to match her hair. She looked so damn beautiful it made my stomach hurt.

I couldn't stop staring at her, taking in every inch of her. It was then I noticed the sky-high shoes she was wearing.

"What the hell are those?"

Bronte looked to where I was pointing. "Shoes. Shoes that you've seen me wear many times."

She was right, I'd seen her wear the bright pink shoes on many occasions, often in my bed, but never when she was pregnant.

"Are you crazy?" I cried. "You could fall off those heels."

The way her eyebrows shot up I knew she thought I was the one who was crazy, not her.

"You want me to hit you with one of them?" Bronte asked, her hands going to her hips.

"No, I want you to sit down before you fall down." I leaned in closer to her. "Don't high shoes give you those big fat blue veins when you're you know?" I nodded toward Bronte's stomach.

"Oh, for God's sake, Carter." My sister sighed. "She's pregnant, not forty-five."

My head shot up as Bronte gasped.

"You said we couldn't tell anyone," I hissed.

"She's my best friend." Bronte's cheeks went pink as she glared at Ellie.

"Oh, my goodness," Hunter whispered, sounding like some sort of robot on crack. "Are you pregnant?"

I looked up at the ceiling and groaned.

"You told Hunter?" Bronte asked, bringing my gaze back to her.

"No, I had no idea." Hunter gasped a little too loudly and Penny's head shot up from cleaning the other end of bar. She stared at us staring at her and when no one spoke, she shrugged and went back to work.

Ellie burst out laughing and leaned into his side. "Oh baby, you are so shit at acting."

"I'm a great actor," he protested. "Be honest, you had no damn clue, did you?"

All three of our gazes snapped to him, each one of us totally shocked he'd even have an inkling of a thought that he was a good actor.

"Dude, you stink. No wonder Jeremy Anderson took your part as Joseph in the nativity."

Hunter hit my stomach with the back of his hand. "We were six you dick."

"Okay so you were six *and shit*." I turned back to Bronte. "I'm sorry I told Hunter, but you told Ellie and she has the biggest mouth."

"I do not," Ellie argued. "I can keep a secret."

"No, you can't," Bronte leaned closer to Ellie and whispered, "You just told Carter that I was pregnant."

Ellie gave me a withering stare. "It's not like he didn't know. He was the one who stuck his thing inside of you and made a baby." My sister grimaced and shook herself.

Turning from Ellie and back to me, Bronte sighed.

"This has to go no further than the four of us for now. I don't want anyone else to know."

Her chin wobbled and she took a deep breath as she glanced over to Penny, who was still busy at the other end of the bar. I knew she was worried, but if she'd just let me be there for her and help to take the strain.

"Lollipop, please just let us go back to my apartment and talk about it."

Bronte shook her head. "Nuh uh. I know you, Carter Maples. You'll get me in that apartment and then dazzle me with that penis of yours."

"Ugh, please." Ellie gagged which made Hunter chuckle.

"Do you two think you could leave us for a few minutes?" I asked, getting more frustrated by the minute.

"They don't need to." Bronte breathed out. "I told you. You need to be sure that you're okay with this."

"I am." I took a step closer to her, desperate to touch her. Anxious to take her into my arms and tell her it would all be okay.

"You fainted when I told you and accused me of lying. How is that being okay with it?"

"You're shitting me," Ellie cried around a laugh. "Please tell me that's true."

"Oh yeah it's true alright," Hunter offered. "He told me himself."

Bronte, clearly having had her fill of the shit talking, snatched up her purse and turned for the door.

"I'm going home. Ellie, you need a ride?"

Ellie grinned at Hunter and then turned back to Bronte. "I'll go with Hunt."

"Bronte, please," I pleaded. "Come back to the apartment. I swear we'll just talk."

She hesitated for a moment, but then with a tired smile shook her head. "I'll call you tomorrow, Carter. I just need sleep right now."

"Are you okay? Is it the shoes, are they making your legs ache? Is the baby lying on your bladder?"

The look she gave me would have killed a lesser man. Even so, it did make me shiver with fear.

"How the hell did you get to be a veterinarian?" she asked. "You really are stupid."

With that she turned on the damn heels and stormed toward the door. I also noticed she had a couple of extra pounds on her ass, which I had to say looked mighty fine. Maybe complimenting her was a way back into her good books.

"Hey, Lollipop?"

She stopped abruptly and I saw her shoulders heave. "What?"

"Your ass looks amazing with a little baby weight."

I swear, if I'd have seen the shoe coming, I would have ducked, but hey the scar on my head would be something to tell the kid about when it was older.

CHAPTER 4

Bronte

If there was one day when I didn't want to be waxing ladies' cooches, today was the day. My argument with Carter the night before was playing on my mind and I could barely concentrate.

I knew he wanted to do what was right, but the right thing wasn't always the best thing.

Of course, I loved Carter, much as I hated admitting it; but the Carter I loved was carefree, fun and spontaneous. It certainly wasn't the grouchy, foul-mouthed, self-centered dick that he was to Ellie, his friends and sometimes his folks. He was different with me, but would he be able to step up and add sensible and responsible to his character? I wasn't so sure.

Sighing heavily, I opened up my appointment book to check who was next in. A back wax for Jim Wickerson, the local pig farmer.

Great. Fuck my life.

Wondering if I had enough disinfectant spray for the treatment bed after

Jim's visit, the door to my salon pushed open. A huge bouquet of pink and white peonies appeared followed by a shock of deep auburn hair.

"Carter," I sighed.

"Hey, Lollipop." He let the door close behind him and poked his head above the flowers, giving me a shy smile.

My damn stomach did a flip, as it always did when he gave me his 'apology grin'. He was so damn cute. I hated him for it.

"I came to say sorry," he said pushing the bouquet toward me.

"They're beautiful. Thank you." I took them from him. "And I'm sorry for throwing my shoe at you. How's your head?"

He shrugged and touched the side of his head. "My mom says where there's no sense there's no feeling, so…"

"You were an idiot," I replied, narrowing my gaze at him.

"I know, but in my defense your ass does look amazing."

Trying not to look at him, seeing as he was much too good at winning me around with his array of smiles, I put the flowers down on the desk.

"Do you have a vase?" he asked. "I can get it for you."

I shook my head. "Lilah is having her lunch and is on a call to her boyfriend. Best leave her alone, they're having issues."

Carter looked a little sheepish as he bit on his bottom lip. "Not just us then."

"Well, I doubt Gary told Lilah she had a fat ass."

"I apologized. And I've seen Lilah, she's real skinny."

Blinking slowly, I tried to compute what he'd just said. "Did you just tell me that Lilah is skinny but I'm fat?"

"What? No, you know I didn't." He threw his hands into the air. "Shit, Lollipop, I just can't win with you."

"No, you can't," I replied, leaning closer to him. "So, you may as well leave."

"I'm not leaving until we sort this." He folded his arms across his broad chest and leaned against the wall, planting himself for the long run by the look of things.

My blood boiled. "I don't want to sort it. In fact, I'd be happy never to set eyes on your stupid face ever again."

Carter grinned and slowly licked his bottom lip, his eyes twinkling, no doubt with some idiotic plan to make me cave.

"Stop looking at me like that," I snapped. "It's not going to work."

Carter's eyes went immediately to my boobs which were heaving pretty rapidly.

"You sure?" he asked.

"Yes," I bit back. "That's pure anger getting my adrenaline going, don't think for one minute it's anything else."

His head cocked to one side as his gaze moved up and down my body. Just having him watch me was a turn on, but I'd be damned if I'd let him know that.

"Sometimes, Carter I wonder how high my mom dropped me."

"I don't understand," he replied, frowning.

"Well, she must have dropped me on my damn head for me to fall for you. You're nothing but a…"

"Pickle stealer?"

He was not laughing at me, was he?

He had a grin on his face, so yes, he was.

"I was thinking more a dirty rotten ball sack," I snarled, moving closer to him, my hands curled into tight fists.

Carter looked at me like I was a toddler who needed to be brought down from a tantrum and that got me madder than a wet hen.

"If you really want to keep your balls, Carter," I said pointing a finger in the region of his stupid, fertile bits and pieces. "I'd suggest that you shut your mouth and get out."

"Ah c'mon Lollipop, don't be like that. I've been reading a Dummy's Guide to becoming a Dad and arguing isn't good for the baby."

"Not good for the baby," I blasted. "You're not good for *my* health, not just the baby's."

Carter sighed. "Please, Lollipop. Take a seat."

Moving behind the reception counter, he pulled out the chair and ushered me toward it.

"No," I screeched, so loud it hurt my ears.

"Lollipop, I-"

"What the hell is going on out here?"

"Oh God," I groaned, dropping my head into my hands. "Mrs. Callahan, I forgot you were in there."

"Shit, Mrs. Callahan," Carter cried. "Your clothes."

Lifting my head, I almost burst a blood vessel when I saw Mrs. Callahan standing with her hands on her hips wearing nothing but the paper panties that I'd given her to wear. Her wrinkly old titties were swinging free, almost reaching her belly button.

"Don't tell me you've never seen a naked body, Carter Maples. Well, I know you have because of the conversation I just heard you yelling." Mrs. Callahan shook her head. "Gotta say I'm shocked. You, a medical person, putting a bun in your girlfriend's belly by accident."

She took a step toward him and as her titties moved from side to side, Carter retched, slapping a hand over his eyes.

"Mrs. Callahan," he groaned. "Your panties have... they're kind of... oh shit."

I looked down to see what he was talking about and sighed.

"Mrs. Callahan, do you want to go back to the treatment room?" I put an arm around her and attempted to guide her back. No one needed to see her cooch hanging out of her panties. "I'll be with you soon to do your massage."

"Ah stop your fussing. There's nothing wrong with a naked woman, especially when she looks after herself." She winked at me and nudged Carter with a bony elbow. "You know it, eh, Carter."

Carter made a noise at the back of his throat and started moving toward the exit door.

"I think I should go, Lollipop."

"Don't go on my account." Mrs. Callahan slid both her thumbs into the sides of the panties and readjusted them, tucking everything back inside. "There you go, the girls are back in the glory hole. You can open your eyes now."

"Oh my God," Carter whimpered.

"You need to remember one thing." The old lady sighed. "You and that right hand of yours are going to get real acquainted when that babe is born. After squeezing it out, your damn appendage is the last thing this little lady will want near her flower garden."

"Shit, someone help me." Carter seemed to physically wither as Mrs. Callahan cackled out a laugh.

"As for you," she continued, pointing at me. "Those perky titties of yours will look like tennis balls in socks, if you're not careful. You need to do plenty of chest exercises; that's what I did."

She looked down at herself and gave a little self-satisfied smile.

"Okay, I'm done," Carter said with an air of finality. "I'll call you later, Lollipop."

As Mrs. Callahan scratched under her armpit, I was too distracted to carry on being mad with him and gave him a sympathetic smile.

"Hey, Carter," Mrs. Callahan called. "You ever need more advice, just hit me up at the gas station. I can always spare time for the young men of Dayton Valley." She winked at his disappearing back and then smiled at me. "So, honey, tell me. Why's he calling you Lollipop?"

I whimpered and wondered whether it would be unprofessional to run and leave Lilah to deal with her.

"I think I know," she replied, finally deciding to go back to the treatment room. "Seeing as my husband Daniel used to call me Queen Fellatio."

"Lilah, I need you now!"

CHAPTER 5

Carter

When I walked into my folk's living room, the last thing I expected to see was my dad sat at an easel, painting. He'd never painted anything in his life, not even a fence post. Anything like that needing doing at home he got decorators in.

"What the hell is going on?" I asked, looking him up and down. "And what the hell are you wearing?"

"If you don't know son," he replied, tilting his head to check out his masterpiece, "then that fancy education of yours was a waste of time. And if you must know it's a smock."

"What the hell is a smock?"

Dad rolled his eyes. "This, you idiot. It's to stop me from getting paint on my clothes. I got vermillion on my shirt yesterday and your mom pitched a real fit."

I didn't even pretend to know what vermillion was. My main concern was that he was wearing what looked like a maternity dress.

Shit – I wondered if maybe Bronte could borrow it when she got bigger?

"What do you want anyway?" Dad asked, always the genial parent glad to see his first-born home. "You're interrupting me while I'm channeling my inner Bob Ross."

I sighed heavily and flopped down onto his armchair which he'd had so long it was pretty much grooved to the shape of his ass. Mom kept trying to get rid of it, even getting a charity who collected furniture to come pick it up at one time. Somehow Dad found out where it had gone and went to their warehouse and actually paid to get it back.

"Spit it out, son," he said, turning to face me. "I have the ethereal glow to do yet and I need to get it just right. I'm struggling getting it to look... well, ethereal."

As he frowned, I second guessed my choice of Henry Maples as my confidante. Maybe Mom would be better, if I could persuade her to keep her mouth closed. Within seconds though I'd rethought the idea, knowing it would never happen and that Dad was my best option.

"You have to promise not to tell Mom," I said leaning forward and narrowing my eyes on him. "I mean it, Dad, she can't find this out, yet."

"I don't keep secrets from your mom, you should know that."

"Shit, you sound as damn pussy whipped as Hunter. Apparently, he doesn't keep secrets from Ellie either."

"Good," Dad said with a nod of his head. "Glad to hear he's treating my baby girl properly. Now come on, spit it out."

The sneaky shit thought I'd tell him without him promising.

"You have to swear, Dad. If you do, I'll tell you."

He sighed heavily and rushed out, "Promisenottotellyourmom."

"Damn, Dad." I grabbed his arm and grinned. "You really are scared of Mom. You played college ball and she's half your size. You could take her down easily."

Dad's eyes widened as he pointed a finger at me. "Do not let that woman fool you. She's scarier than you can possibly know. You and Ellie have only ever seen her sweet side."

I began to laugh; he looked genuinely scared. "Mom is all sugar. There's not one tiny bit of sour in her."

"You've never eaten her last Pop Tart."

"Mom doesn't eat Pop Tarts," I argued. "Too much refined sugar."

"Not now, but in college she did. I suffered for a whole three days because of it."

Pinching the bridge of my nose, I groaned quietly.

"You know, maybe I'll go and speak to Mr. Bridges," I replied, getting up from the chair.

"Mr. Bridges is in a coma, isn't he?"

"Yeah, he is, but he also isn't scared of his wife twenty years after stealing her last damn Pop Tart. I also think I'll get more sense out of him."

Dad glared and then swung sideways on his stool so that he was facing me fully. "I give great advice, just ask your sister. Now spill it."

Chewing on my bottom lip I contemplated if I was doing the right thing. Maybe I should have spoken to Hunter and kept our imminent arrival between the four of us who already knew.

"Is Lance finally going to retire and put you in charge?" Dad asked, dropping his paintbrush into a jar of water and then leaning back to take another look at his masterpiece.

"No, and I think I'll retire before he does as this rate. Which is why I'm gonna ask him to let me become partner."

Dad looked impressed as he wiped his hands on his smock. "Good idea. Do you need money for that, is that what you want to talk about?"

"No," I sighed. "I have that covered."

He brought his gaze back to mine and shrugged. "Okay, well what then? 'Cause I gotta tell you son, the damn suspense is killing me."

"You swear you won't tell Mom?" I questioned, rubbing my sweaty palms together.

He didn't answer but was definitely thinking about it; the look on his face was like he was passing a kidney stone.

"Dad!"

"I said I wouldn't, didn't I? Now just get on with it." He huffed impatiently and then turned momentarily back to his canvas. "Gotta say, son, it's good, don't you think?"

I took my first real look at the picture and did a double take.

"Fuck, Dad, please tell me that isn't Mom's naked body."

He grinned and then winked.

"What is wrong with you?" I cried, throwing my hands into the air. "You're determined to scar me for life." My head whipped around the room. "Where the hell is she? If you're painting her why isn't she in the room?"

"I drew her yesterday, now I'm painting her." He started to mess around with his paints, turning his back on me.

Not wanting to waste another minute, I blew out a long breath.

"Okay," I said, getting his attention. "You ready?"

He nodded, swinging back around to me. "Go ahead."

I cleared my throat. "Bronte's pregnant and has dumped me and I have no idea what to do."

Dad reared back on his stool. "What the actual fuck?"

"Yeah, you heard right."

"Shit, son," he replied, pushing up from his stool and moving toward me. "That's some damn big news."

The shock was evident as Dad placed a hand on my shoulder and blinked rapidly.

"I suppose me giving you a lecture about birth control is pointless," he said puffing out his cheeks.

"Kind of late, yeah."

We stood in silence and it must only have been for a few seconds but felt like hours as my dad watched me carefully; his inquisitive blue eyes searching my face.

"I know we brought you up to be responsible," he finally said. "So, I hope you're asking me how to get Bronte to see that."

I nodded. "Yes sir. Exactly that."

"Good boy." He pulled me into a hug and his large hand patted my back. "Congratulations."

"You're not angry at me?" I asked as he gave me a tight squeeze.

He pulled away from me and shook his head. "Not going to lie, I think you're an idiot for not tying Lance down about the partnership first. You should have settled your future before bringing another life into this world. And I'm sure you know that Jim and Darcy won't be happy that you got their little girl in the family way."

"Yeah, I know." My heart thudded as I thought about that conversation. I loved Bronte, but our situation didn't bode well for us making things work. Her parents were probably going to quite rightly pitch a fit about it. "I want us to be a family, Dad."

"Bronte's not so keen though?" Dad moved over to his chair and indicated for me to take a seat on the couch. "Did you do something for her to doubt you?"

"No! I love her, I want this." I thought about the conversations we'd had since she'd told me the news. "Maybe I haven't always said the right thing to her, but I've made it clear I want us to do it together."

"Seems like not saying the right things has finally caught up with you then." He rolled his eyes. "I love you more than life, Carter. But sometimes, son, you're a damn idiot whose mouth shoots off before his damn brain has engaged."

He wasn't wrong.

"So, any advice?" I asked, not wishing to dwell on my stupid mouth.

"First off you need to prove to her you're serious about actually being an adult. First thing in the morning, you speak to Lance about the partnership and if he tries to put you off then maybe you should consider setting up on your own."

I blew out a breath. "Shit, Dad, that's a lot of responsibility."

"Yeah, well that's what being a parent is all about, son. You have to provide for your family. If Lance isn't willing to give you that then you have to have a plan B."

"And getting myself into debt to set up my own practice is a good plan B?"

He considered me for a few seconds and then nodded. "Yeah, it is. If that's what you decide, then Mom and I will help you out with a loan. We have savings and some shares that we can cash in."

"No, no way. That's yours' and Mom's retirement fund. I'm not taking that from you."

"Well, we ain't retiring yet, no matter how old you think we are. Besides," he said leaning forward and resting his arms on his knees. "We have enough for both."

My eyes went wide. I had no idea my folks were so well off. Then again, Dad had realized at an early age how your future could change at the snap of an ACL. He'd evidently made sure since then that his family would be okay, no matter what happened.

"As for Bronte, you just have to keep telling her how you feel and that you want this baby. Keep telling and showing her and eventually, if she loves you, she'll come around. She does love you right?"

If he'd asked me that a couple of weeks before I'd have said yes, but recently I wasn't so sure.

"I think so," I answered with a heavy weight in my chest. "I think maybe being pregnant has clouded her judgment a little."

"Believe me son, do not say that to her. Never tell a woman that hormones are making her crazy." He studied me, realization dawning on his face. "Oh fuck, Carter, you idiot."

"I guess you're right about my mouth shooting off before my brain has kicked in."

"Okay," Dad said and pinched the bridge of his nose. "First speak to Lance and at least try and show your pregnant ex-girlfriend that you're attempting to be an adult."

"Oh my God, I'm going to be a grandma!"

Mom came rushing into the living room wearing just a robe and a huge damn smile on her face.

"Mom," I cried. "Have you been listening in?"

Ignoring my question, she rushed over and practically threw herself at me, wrapping her slim arms around my neck.

"My baby is having a baby. Oh sweetheart, I'm so happy for you."

"Melinda, honey," Dad sighed. "You're not supposed to listen in on private conversations, you know that."

Mom extricated herself from me and turned to Dad. "Oh, you'd have told me later anyway. You know you would."

"He promised," I protested.

"Son, I swear, I would never."

Mom waved him away and plonked herself next to me and took my hand in hers. "He would've sweetheart; you know he would. Now, tell me is Bronte taking her vitamins and when is her due date? Is she going to move into the apartment with you?"

"Well, you obviously weren't listening that carefully," Dad said. "Bronte had dumped his ass."

Mom gasped and looked between me and Dad before finally settling her gaze on me.

"What for?"

Shrugging I said, "I think she thinks I feel obliged."

"And do you?" Mom's eyes were hard and steely, daring me not to shame her.

"No, Mom. Of course, I don't. I love her. I want us to be a family."

Mom sniffed and turned to Dad. "Oh Henry, how beautiful is our boy?"

"Yeah, beautiful and fertile," Dad replied.

"That's what I wanted to speak to Dad about." I told Mom. "I wanted to know how to get her back."

Mom gave me some sort of dreamy smile that I normally only saw after they'd had 'alone time'. "Oh, your dad is real good with the ladies. I bet he gave you some great advice."

Closing my eyes, I shuddered. My parents had to be the weirdest fucking people on the planet. They were sex crazy at forty-eight years of age. It wasn't right.

"I should call Darcy," Mom said excitedly, bringing me back from my nightmare thoughts.

"No," I cried. "You can't. Bronte hasn't told her folks yet. We agreed to wait. You can't let her know that you know. Promise me, Mom."

Mom's promises I trusted, so much more than Dad's. I knew she could keep a secret. She'd kept the fact that Ellie and I had broken Dad's great-aunt's vase, the one holding her ashes, from him for years. He still thought they were in a safe place and that the stuff in the jar in the cupboard under the stairs was bath salts of some kind.

"I swear," she replied. "But they're going to have to find out soon."

"Yeah, I know, but that's Bronte's call, okay?"

Mom nodded and leaned in to kiss my cheek. "We'll help you fix things with her."

I wasn't sure how keen I was on that, but I probably needed all the help I could get. Contemplating it, my phone buzzed in my pocket. I pulled it out to find a text from Alaska which opened up a picture of a woman's hand with a square diamond on her ring finger and the words 'she said yes'.

"Ah fuck," I groaned. "That's all I need."

"What is it?" Mom asked, peering over at my phone.

Another text came in telling me that he was having a party in three weeks' time for his and Jen's engagement party.

"More loved up couples," I said and showed it to Mom.

"Oh, my goodness, that's so exciting and he did good with that ring." She grabbed the phone from me to take a closer look. "That's it," she cried. "That's how you get Bronte back. Ask her to marry you."

She stared between Dad and me with a starry-eyed smile and we both moaned in unison, knowing for a fact that this was one of those occasions when she wouldn't take no for an answer.

CHAPTER 6

Bronte

Watching another couple be all in love and shit was not what I'd call a good night out. My heart felt heavy and aside from the baby in my tummy, it felt kind of empty – pretty much like the rest of me. I missed Carter and just wanted to be at home wallowing in my sadness.

Alaska and Jennifer were good friends though, and not turning up would've been just rude. Hence, why I was sitting at a high table in Stars & Stripes with a glass of coke looking like the cheese had fallen off my cracker.

"Your mom and dad are going to notice if you don't smile." Ellie nudged me with her elbow as her mouth chased after the straw in her drink. "I'm guessing you still haven't told them."

"Nope." I kept my gaze fixed firmly ahead. "It's not the right time."

I could feel Ellie's eyes on me and knew she was staring me down. Well, that game didn't work unless you were both looking at each other, so that spoiled her fun.

"When will that be?" she finally asked. "When you're pushing a stroller around? Or when your mom wants to know why you can't fit into those tiny denim shorts that you always insist on wearing on Saturdays whatever the weather?"

"Do not," I bit out. "I only wear them during the summer."

"Bullshit." Ellie put her glass down on the table, if a little forcefully. "You wore them to the Christmas Fete and your legs were almost as blue as your hair is now."

"Ellie," I sighed. "You're getting on my last nerve. Where the hell is your boyfriend to take you away from me so he can fuck you around the back somewhere?"

"He and his dad are talking to Jason Miller. And just so you know, we would not 'fuck around the back somewhere' at someone else's engagement party."

I snorted because I truly doubted that. They were damn insatiable for each other.

"Where's *your* boyfriend, anyway?"

My head snapped around to face Ellie. "Well, that's just plain nasty," I replied, giving her the stink eye.

She laughed and pulled me into her side for a hug. "Got you to actually look at me though, didn't I?"

I rolled my eyes and sighed. "I guess. Where is your brother anyway?"

Ellie shrugged. "No idea. He is coming though because he bought himself a new shirt especially for the occasion."

"That man has more shirts than there are days in a year, I'm sure of it." The idea of Carter's shirts made me smile. He kept them in color order in his closet and never wore the same one twice in one month.

"Seriously though," Ellie ventured. "When are you going to tell your mom and dad?"

A pain thudded in my temples and I wished that I could just run and hide for the next seven months. My pregnancy wasn't something I wanted to face with my mom and dad. Once I did it would be real and just another problem to add to their worries.

"I have no idea," I replied. "They're going to counselling and have enough shit to deal with."

Ellie opened her mouth and took a deep breath, no doubt ready to give me another of her pearls of wisdom, but I cut her off.

"I know that you think they'll be great about it and welcome a grandchild, but I can't be sure about that, El. As much as my mom will probably be as happy as a hog in mud about a grandbaby, it's hardly what she would have wanted for me; twenty-four and unmarried with a bun in the oven. Carter may also find himself on my dad's shit list."

Ellie nodded and exhaled. "You know best and I'm sorry I keep trying to tell you what to do. It's your decision."

She pulled me in for a hug and squeezed me tight and I felt my body finally relax.

"Thank you," I whispered, looking over her shoulder and seeing Carter walking toward us. "Oh shit, your brother looks hot."

Ellie let me go and turned. "Well, if you like that kind of thing."

"I really do," I groaned.

Moving purposefully toward us, Carter looked so damn yummy I was pretty sure there was drool on my chin. He was wearing grey dress pants and a purple dress shirt which clung to his muscular arms and chest. It was tucked into the pants and showed off his narrow waist and slim hips to perfection. Even his hair looked hot, swept back with a piece hanging sexily in front of his hazel eyes.

"Ladies." He kissed us both on the cheek. "Looking lovely."

Ellie frowned and felt Carter's forehead. "You ill or high?"

"No, I'm not ill and I haven't had time to get high. I only finished sewing Mr. Calhoun's dog's ball back into its nut sack an hour ago. Then I had to go home shave, shower and shi... well you get the picture."

"Something's wrong," Ellie retorted. "You're being nice to me."

"I can be nice," Carter protested. "Can't I, Lollipop?"

Choosing not to answer, I took a sip of my coke and watched as Ellie and Carter broke out into a fight of knuckles.

"Please stop," I sighed. "This is an engagement party, not a fifth birthday."

Carter gave Ellie a little nudge. "Sorry, Lollipop."

"Shit, where did your balls go?" Ellie muttered.

"Same place as your personality, apparently." Carter gave her a smirk and then turned his attention back to me. "You think you should have a comfier seat than that stool?" he asked.

"Not really, no."

"Well, I do." He looked around the room. "There, that one looks real comfy. I'll get it for you."

"Carter," Ellie cried. "You can't do that Jennifer's grandma is sitting on it."

Eighty-five-year-old, Mrs. McGillicuddy was seated on a high-back, plump, red velvet chair, surrounded by her four children and various grandchildren and great-grandchildren. She was in a prime spot, enabling her to watch the party carrying on around her.

"She can find another seat," Carter said.

"She's old, Carter," I objected.

"And you're pregnant," he replied, thankfully lowering his voice. "I think a pregnant woman trumps an old lady."

"I don't. So just leave me on my stool and Mrs. McGillicuddy on her throne."

He let out a breath through his nostrils and pouted. "Fine, but at least let me get you another coke."

"Okay, thank you."

I passed him my glass as Ellie shoved hers at him too.

"Vodka and diet please." She gave him a sweet and sickly smile. "Also, can you rescue Hunter and Jefferson from Jason, please. You know how he bores them both to sleep."

Carter picked up our glasses. "I'll rescue Jefferson, but I may just leave Hunter there. Payback for all the shit he does to me."

"What shit?" Ellie asked.

"Dating you for a start, because you do know if you ever get married, I'll be the best man."

"And?" I asked, noticing that Ellie's cheeks had gone a beautiful shade of pink.

"It means I'll have to be nice to her for a whole day. Who the hell says shit to a bride on her wedding day?" Carter replied with a shrug of his shoulders and walked off to the bar.

"And you wonder why I don't think he's ready to be a father," I sighed watching his perfect ass walk away from me.

***

"Are you sure you don't want a foot rub?" Carter asked for the tenth time.

"No, I told you," I hissed. "I'm fine.

He, along with Hunter, Ellie and everyone else at the damn party were drunk; even my folks had been two-stepping together. Carter though was particularly drunk and had been wobbling a little too much.

"What about a titty rub then?" he asked with a grin.

Hunter almost spat out his beer. "Oh, shit buddy, you're in so much trouble now."

"Sorry." Carter giggled like a twelve-year-old girl and took another drink of his whisky.

"Don't be too hard on him though, Bronte," Hunter added. "He didn't eat any buffet."

"No, don't stop her," Ellie said, wrapping herself around Hunter, demanding his attention. "It'd be good to see her ripping him a new one."

Hunter laughed and immediately fused his mouth with Ellie's—it was becoming clear that alcohol had made them hornier than usual.

"How about *you* give *me* a little kiss?" Carter's lips puckered like a cat's behind as his kissy face loomed toward me. "Just a little one, because I know you love me."

"Carter no, you stink of booze and it's making me feel nauseous." I held a palm in front of his face.

"Ah give him one kiss," Hunter said, pulling his lips away from Ellie's.

"How the hell could you hear that?" I asked, still wrestling Carter away from smelling distance. "You were having your lips suctioned off by Ellie."

Hunter grinned. "I can multitask."

"Since when?" Carter asked, grabbing a hold of the table to stop himself from falling.

"I can eat Ellie out and whistle at the same time."

"Oh baby," Ellie sighed, looking up at him as if the sun shone from his ass.

"Oh, sweet Jesus, you're disgusting." I slapped a hand at Hunter's chest, but he merely grinned and went back to sucking off Ellie's face.

"I did not want to know that." Carter hiccupped. "That's my sister."

"You're all a disgrace. You're too drunk and they're too horny. I can't cope with y'all without alcohol."

Carter gasped. "No. You can't drink."

"I don't intend to, you idiot. What do you think I am?"

"I think," he replied on a hiccup. "You're the most beautiful woman I ever met, and I just wished you loved me like Ellie loves Hunter."

His lips pouted and his gorgeous hazel eyes were a little shiny – probably through alcohol, but even so he looked adorable and I felt bad. I only had to say the word and I knew he'd fuck me to heaven and back and we'd be good. Problem was, I had a baby to consider.

"I do love you." I ran a hand down his chest and let out a breath. "But you know I have to be sure it's what you want."

Carter nodded slowly and then leaned in and gave me a chaste kiss to my cheek. As he pulled away his face lit up and I just knew something monumental had crossed his mind.

"I'm so serious about this," he said, narrowing his eyes and nodding. "And I'm going to show you."

"C-Carter," I stammered. "What are you going to do?"

Before I had a chance to grab a hold of him, he turned and started to plough through the people on the dancefloor. Shoving and pushing them out of the way.

"Oh, shit. Hunter, stop him!"

Hunter looked up from his make out session, slightly dazed. "What?"

"Carter's about to do something stupid," I said, jumping down from my stool and chasing after him.

Pushing through people, I almost caught a hold of his arm until Henry and Melinda, doing some outlandish synchronized dance to Mylie Cyrus's

Party in the USA, blocked my way. As they shimmied their shoulders together and then kicked their legs up with a whoop, it was more than obvious which genes ran through Carter and Ellie's DNA.

"Excuse me, I need to get through," I yelled above the music but when they obviously couldn't hear me, I made a quick diversion past them. I was too late though because Carter was taking the mic from Crazy Mike the DJ.

"What's going on?" Hunter asked, coming up beside me.

Pointing to Crazy Mike, who had a mass of wild, grey hair and a pink beard which reached his chest, Hunter followed my gaze and cursed. Carter was tapping the mic' as Crazy Mike turned down the music.

"Please try and stop him, Hunter."

Hunter nodded and continued forward, but as he put out a hand to grab Carter, he ducked the other side of the DJ console.

"Hey everyone," he shouted. "Can I have your attention, please." There was a screeching noise and Crazy Mike leaned across to pull the microphone away from the sexy red head's stupid big mouth.

"Hey," I heard Alaska call from behind me. "You doing a congratulatory toast or something?"

Carter paused and grimaced. "Sorry, no man, but erm yeah, congratulations."

"Well thanks, seeing as this is *our* engagement party."

I turned to speak to Alaska to find him grinning and Jennifer hanging off his arm, gazing up at him.

"Alaska," I called. "Get him down. It's rude."

"Oh, it's fine," he replied. "As long as he doesn't take all night, 'cause I kinda want to say something about my girl." He then dropped his head and began making out with Jennifer and I knew he had no care in the world about Carter taking over.

Turning back to face my damn baby daddy, I felt my stomach roll as once again he dodged Hunter's grasp.

"So, I have something to say," he continued. "Y'all ever heard of a Jackpot Screwer?" He looked around his audience, but apart from a few people muttering, no one answered. "Well okay. It's someone who sleeps with someone to get pregnant—"

"Carter Maples, don't you dare." My heart dropped to my boots, but Carter just grinned back at me.

"What the hell is he doing up there?" I heard Jefferson ask.

"No idea," Henry replied. "But I wonder if he's about to make a big mistake. Son, come on down."

"Anyway," Carter continued, ignoring his dad. "Like I said, it's someone who sleeps with someone else purposefully to get pregnant. But in my case, I just want you to know it's totally different. It's different in my case, because *I'm* the Jackpot Screwer."

I groaned and dropped my head to my hands, hoping to every Lord above that he wasn't going to say what I thought he was.

"And that's because every damn time I hit the jackpot. Every damn time I ring my Lollipop's bells." He then kissed his knuckles and pointed, liked he'd just scored a Superbowl touchdown and was dedicating it to me. "Isn't that right, Lollipop?"

"Why's he calling her Lollipop?" I heard his dad ask as my dad made a strange noise that sounded like he was in pain.

"I'll tell you when we get home, honey," Melinda replied around a cough.

Carter, unaware of the conversation, carried on. "But it's not just about giving it to her good, I hit another jackpot too—"

"No! Don't you dare."

My shout had him looking in my direction, but with a slight wobble to his step he then moved out of my eyeline.

"Ladies and gentlemen, I just need you to know that my little swimmers hit that spot and I put a bun in my Lollipop's oven."

As I looked down and wished the ground would swallow me up, a few people muttered congratulations amidst a smattering of applause, but I think generally everyone was as shocked as I was. Henry cursed, Melinda groaned, my mom gasped… and as for my dad well I'm pretty sure he growled like a grizzly. Carter though, never one to know when to shut his mouth kept on talking.

"So, Lollipop I want you to know, I'm ready for this. I'm ready to be a father and I vote we call our baby Blake, after the most beautiful woman I know."

It was then for the second time in a matter of days that I threw my shoe at Carter's head.

CHAPTER 7

Bronte

Dad paced up and down while Mom stared at me, just as she had been for the last half hour since we'd arrived home from the party.

"What about your business?" Dad asked, mid pace. "You've worked hard, Dayton Valley ladies were not known for their high grooming standards until you started up."

"I've always kept myself tidy," Mom chipped in, the first words she'd spoken since we'd walked through the door. "But Dad is right. What about the salon?"

I rolled my eyes. "Women can be mothers *and* businesswomen at the same time you know. I don't have to be chained to the kitchen sink."

"We know, honey," Mum sighed. "But you have to understand this is a big shock to us. And to find out *that* way."

"You're not kidding," Dad cried. "I'm not ready to even believe you're out of your training bra yet."

"Well, hate to break it to you, Dad, but I had a twenty-fifth birthday a week ago."

And hadn't that been as dull as Henry's bone. Just a family dinner where I'd pretended to have a migraine as an excuse why I hadn't gone out partying with Ellie.

"Doesn't mean I'm ready for my baby to have a baby." Dad threw his hands in the air and went back to pacing.

"Who's having a baby?"

Austen, my little brother, appeared in the doorway of the kitchen, rubbing a hand through his dark blond bed hair. His pajama pants were halfway up his legs and his top was pulled tight across his chest. He'd filled out and shot up over the last couple of months and was growing out of his cute boyish features and looking more like our brother, Shaw; tall and handsome.

We all stared at him, no sound except for that of our breathing.

"What are you doing up, honey?" Mom asked, standing and going to him. "You were fast asleep when we got home."

"Yeah, only because you made me have a sitter and do you know how boring Patty Donahue is? She bored me to sleep." He pretended to yawn which made me laugh, but he was right, Patty Donahue was boring. She collected pencils for goodness sake.

"Well at least we know *you* weren't doing anything you shouldn't be," Dad said with a grunt. "Unlike your sister."

"*Dad!*"

He threw his arms up. "But you have."

"No, I haven't," I protested. "Having sex is the most natural thing in the world. You and Mom have had sex."

"Ugh," Austen groaned. "Please don't."

"Honey, you know what sex is?" Mom asked, running a hand down my brother's hair.

"Duh. I'm fifteen."

"You're fourteen, son," Dad corrected.

"Fourteen, fifteen, it's practically the same," Austen said with a shoulder shrug. "But yes, Mom, I do know what sex is. We have sex ed at school and like I said, I'm fifteen."

"Have you *had* sex?" Mom asked.

Austen slammed his hands over his face. "Oh my God, Mom. *No*, just don't ask me that."

"Austen," Dad growled in a warning tone. "Please tell me that you've not done anything stupid."

I started to giggle. "Really, does he look like he'd know what to do?"

The three of us stared at him in his Transformer pjs with his hot chocolate moustache.

"Yeah, you kind of have a point," Dad sighed and turned to Mom. "I think we're good with kid number three providing us with any surprises of the baby nature, Darce."

Mom gave a sigh of relief. "Okay, honey. You need to get back to bed. We have to speak to Bronte about some things."

"Have you had sex with Carter?" Austen asked, his eyes wide and his mouth gaping as he waited for my response. "Mom, has she had sex with Carter?"

"I'm twenty-five, Austin. What do you think?"

He grinned. "Damn, you're in trouble now."

"Austen," Mom chastised. "Don't say damn."

"Son." Dad sighed. "Just go back to bed." He leaned forward and kissed Austen's hair before turning him and pushing him back toward his bedroom.

"Hey, Dad," he said pulling on Dad's arm. "Are you staying here tonight?"

Dad took a deep breath. "No, I'm going to get an Uber back to my apartment. Now, go to bed."

"I'm always sent to bed," Austen complained as he dragged his feet. "I never get to hear the good stuff. Like when Shaw got caught feeling up Patty Donahue. I was just sent to bed that night too."

"No way," I cried, making a grab for Austen's arm. "Stop, tell me all about it."

Austen turned and started to laugh. "Last summer when Mom and Dad got Patty to sit, Shaw came home a day early and when I went to bed, he and Patty got down and dirty."

"Austen," Dad yelled. *"Bed. Now."*

"What, that's what happened?" he remonstrated, allowing Dad to turn him toward his room again.

"Why did I not know this?" I asked.

"Because," Dad said, throwing Austen a warning glare. "It wasn't important."

"So, he was just feeling her up?" I called.

Austen continued walking. "One hand up her shirt the other down her pants," he called without turning around. "On Mom's new sofa."

I burst out laughing and watched my little brother wander back to bed, leaving my parents to deal with their other errant child – the one who'd got herself knocked up.

"Okay." I sighed and flopped down onto the sofa that now felt kind of dirty. "Go for it. Tell me what a disappointment I am and how I've ruined my life."

Mom sat next to me and placed a cool hand on my forearm. "We don't think either of those things, honey. It's just such a shock. I mean you and Carter being together in itself is huge, but having a baby together, well…"

"Mom's right, sweetheart," Dad said, starting to pace again. "A few short months ago you hated each other. Now you're bringing a new life into the world; together."

I nodded, understanding their worry. Carter and I seemed like a real bad idea on paper. We didn't have a great track record of even being amicable with each other and now we were having a child.

"I understand how it must look," I replied. "But I swear, we do love each other, and I won't let this change what I want to do with my life."

"So, if you love each other, why aren't you still a couple?" Mom asked. "You've barely been together a few months and have already parted. Doesn't look like you have this figured out so well, does it?"

She was right, it wasn't a good sign for our future. "Lots of kids have parents who are apart. Look at us."

Dad narrowed his eyes on me. "Your mom and I are sorting through things and we've been married twenty-five years."

"Twenty-six, Jim," Mom corrected.

Dad winced and rubbed a hand down his face. "Twenty-six, sorry. You've already fallen at the first hurdle, sweetheart."

"I just want to be sure me and a baby are what he wants," I replied.

I also needed to be sure I wasn't going to end up like my mom; crying about my man leaving one day.

"You know what he's like; a big stupid idiot," I stated.

He really was, but the thought of the big stupid idiot still made me smile.

"I know he thinks he wants this," I continued. "But I want him to be sure about it, because if he changes his mind after a few months or even a year, that would be so much worse."

Mom's bright grey eyes shone with understanding because she knew exactly how that felt, the thought of losing the man you loved after you'd built a life together.

"Okay, honey," she replied, giving my hand a squeeze. "Whatever happens we're here for you." She looked up at Dad who was watching her carefully. The look on his face so soft and gentle it stole my breath. "Right, Jim?'

Dad nodded. "Yeah. Always. Whether Carter comes along for the ride or not, you've always got our support."

He engulfed me and Mom in his arms and I knew everything would be okay, one way or another.

CHAPTER 8

Carter

There aren't many things that I regretted in my life but getting drunk on whisky without any food in my belly, is one of my biggest.

In the three days since my drunk-ass announcement Bronte had refused to speak to me even when I returned her shoe; she just snatched it from me and then slammed the door in my face.

Sighing at my own stupidity, I walked out into the waiting room to call for my next patient. We were real busy, it seemed nearly every pet in Dayton Valley had an ailment of some kind.

"Ariana Grande," I called out and when Dulcie Rogers stood up with her mother and a cute looking puppy, I mentally high-fived myself.

The staff and I had a monthly sweepstake on the names of the new puppies and kittens that we would see. They were usually named after popstars or film stars and I'd chosen Ariana as my monthly pick. If no one else's choice came up in the last three days of the month, I'd bagged myself a six-pack of beer as the prize. Okay, so it was a shit prize if three of you won and had to share, but we had fun with it.

"Okay, Dulcie, so we're giving Ariana her puppy injections today, right?" I asked as Dulcie and her mom Vivien closed the door of my consulting room behind them.

"It's actually *Ariana Grande*," Dulcie informed me as she placed the French Bulldog on the examination table."

"My bad," I replied and grinned at Vivien.

If I'd expected her to laugh along with me about her daughter's fussiness over her dog's name, I'd have been mistaken. Her face was sour enough to curdle milk. Schooling my features back into something more professional, I set about getting everything ready. As I went about my job and soothed the puppy before sticking a needle into her, Vivien tsked real loud and followed it up with a sigh. I might have ignored it had she not muttered, "A total embarrassment," under her breath loud enough for me to hear.

"Okay," I said brightly and turned to Dulcie. "All done. If you want to take her to see Louisa on the reception desk, I'm sure she's got a treat Ariana Grande can have."

Dulcie gave me a huge smile and carefully picked up the puppy, cradling it like a baby. Vivien went to follow Dulcie, but I stopped her by calling her name.

"Yes," she said, narrowing her eyes on me.

"Have you got a problem, Vivien? Because if you have, I'd rather you tell me."

"Do I have a problem?" she asked, folding her arms over her ample chest. "Of course, I have a problem; you. Embarrassing poor Bronte like that."

I groaned and rubbed a hand down my face. It was bad enough Bronte and her folks being at outs with me, but the rest of the town as well?

"I'm not proud of myself, Vivien. I had too much to drink and let my mouth run away with me. I've apologized to Bronte along with her mom and dad, there's not much more I can do."

Vivien arched a brow and made a move toward the door. "Maybe grow up and show her you're ready to be a father."

"I don't think—"

She didn't hear what else I had to say, because she walked away and pulled the door closed behind her.

"Fuck," I groaned and threw my pen across the room.

Vivien was right, I had to prove to Bronte that I was ready to be a dad. First thing I needed to do in my mission, was to speak to Lance. Going through the door at the back of my consulting room, I strode off to find him. As expected, he was in the office doing paperwork.

"You put an invoice in for your time at Wickerson's last week?"

"Afternoon to you too, Lance. And yes, I did it yesterday."

He looked up and grunted something before bending his head back to his desk and continuing to write in his big ledger.

"Lance, I've told you, I can get all of that put onto the computer."

"And I told you, ain't nothing wrong with a good old-fashioned pen and ledger," he replied, still not looking up at me. "Now have you just come in here to drag me into the twenty-first century, or was there something else?"

Taking a deep breath, I pulled the guest chair out from his desk and sat down. We'd had many versions of the conversation to come, but the time had arrived for me to give him an ultimatum.

"I guess you heard that me and Bronte are having a baby."

"Yup."

I still got no eye contact but carried on regardless.

"That means I need to think a bit more about my future. I need to be sure my family are well taken care of."

"From what I heard you'll be lucky if Bronte ever talks to you again, never mind want to set up a family situation with you."

"Yeah, she's mad." I sighed, frustrated that he was still writing damn numbers down. "Hopefully, she'll forgive me."

"And how do you propose to get her to do that?" he asked, finally lifting his head.

I leaned forward, resting my forearms on my thighs, wanting Lance to see the desire in my eyes.

"I want partner," I replied, my voice strong and steady. "I have the money and I think I'm ready. You're not going to retire and let me run the business any time soon, so I figure I should buy in. It's a win, win situation."

"And how do you work that out?" Lance put his pen into the crease of the ledger pages and sat back, waiting for the sales pitch that he would have no choice but to accept.

"I get the responsibility I want, while you get some cash but still get to carry on working."

He never said much but I knew the big old house he lived in on the outskirts of town ate up a lot of his money. He'd told me once he wanted to sell it, but his wife wouldn't hear of it. Their son Martin had been born there and as he'd been killed in Iraq, the house held a lot of memories for Dorothy and now she couldn't stand to leave it.

Lance's eyes narrowed and he let out a slow breath. I'd definitely piqued his interest.

"Let me think about it," he replied. "Chat to Dorothy."

I wanted to do a little jig in my seat because if he was talking to Dorothy, he was serious about it.

"Appreciate it, Lance. I really -."

"Vet required urgently. We have a cat that has been involved in an RTA."

The speaker system blasted out, making us both jump in our seats. I was on my feet first.

"I'll go."

Rushing into the reception the last person I expected to see was Bronte, cradling Roderick against her. Jim was with her and had his arm around her shoulders.

"Carter," Bronte cried and ran straight to me. "A car hit him and drove off. He got up but was dragging his leg."

"Shit. Okay, quick follow me."

When we got into my consulting room, I got Bronte to lay Roderick on the table, while I pushed a button to call one of the nurses to come and help.

"Is he going to be okay?" Bronte cried as she watched me feel around her cat.

"Don't worry, Lollipop, he's in the best place now."

Jessica, one of our nurses stepped inside and gasped when she saw

Bronte.

"Oh God, what happened?"

"RTA," I explained. "Can you hold him while I check his back legs."

Over the next couple of minutes, Jessica and I did what we needed to be done while Bronte and Jim watched on in shocked silence. When I was finally happy with my examination, I gave Roderick a sedative and asked Jessica to take him for an x-ray.

"Okay," I said as Jessica left the room. "I'm confident nothing is broken, but we'll soon find out for sure. Even so, he's real lucky. You see who hit him?" I asked. "It wasn't Ellie was it, you know trying to get us to talk?"

I laughed loudly at my own joke but was faced with two blank faces.

"Okay, too soon," I muttered, remembering when my sister had given the damn cat laxatives to try and get me and Bronte together—even though secretly we already were. "So, I'll get him x-rayed and then let you know what the situation is. If he hasn't got any broken bones, I'm still going to keep him in."

"Why?" Bronte asked, her bottom lip quivering.

Running a hand down her arm, I gave her what I hoped was a comforting smile. "I just want to observe him, check his bladder and bowels are working okay and that the impact hasn't damaged them."

When Bronte whimpered, Jim pulled her into his side. "Hey come on now. Like Carter said, he's in the best place."

"You sure you think he'll be okay?"

"Lollipop, I wouldn't lie to you."

As my eyes met hers, I felt the usual electricity between us. How her existence in the same air space as me, made my heart thud and the blood rush in my ears. She was so damn beautiful with her blue hair in little buns either side of her head adding cute to the sexiness. It was difficult to believe I used to hate the sight of her until one night in Stars & Stripes we'd had a drunken kiss.

We must have been looking at each other pretty intensely because when Jim cleared his throat, we both jumped.

"I'll go and erm…" He pointed to the door. "I'll wait outside for you, sweetheart."

Neither of us spoke until we heard the door click shut behind him.

"I'm sorry," I burst out. "I was a drunken idiot and I'll never forgive myself."

Bronte shook her head. "It's fine. At least they know now. Well, them and the rest of the damn town." She gave me a small smile and I was happy that she appeared to have forgiven me a little bit. "Just next time you drink whisky, maybe eat food too."

"Yeah, I will."

Inhaling deeply, I felt unusually lost for words. Not lost as such but scared. I was damn petrified in case I said the wrong thing and pissed her off again— that was how tentative I knew our truce to be.

"You're feeling okay?" I asked, thinking it was a pretty neutral question.

"I'm fine. Tired like you wouldn't believe, but I read that's natural for the first trimester."

"You take as much rest as you can." I was desperate to take her into my arms and kiss her but was pretty sure we weren't at that point. I settled for holding her hand instead. "You need anything?"

Bronte shook her head and looked down at our linked hands. At first, I thought she was going to pull hers free so was surprised when she placed her other hand over the top.

"I have a doctor's appointment on Friday, if you want to come with?"

This was good. I'd obviously done and said the right things if she wanted me with her. Maybe going to the appointment would be my opportunity to turn things around and prove I was serious and committed.

"I'd love to," I replied feeling confident I had everything under control. "Although you know I could grease up my arm and check everything out for you myself. I do it with Hunter's cows all the damned time."

CHAPTER 9

Bronte

D riving along with my windows down and Lizzo's *'Juice'* playing on the radio my shoulders felt a little lighter. Knowing that Mom and Dad weren't madder than a pair of wet hens about becoming grandparents was a big relief. The talk we'd had after the *incident* had shown me that they were the best parents ever and all was good in the hood.

As for Carter, well he was a different story entirely. My anger at what he did at the party had subsided, he was taking good care of my cat after all, but I was still unsure what to do about him—about us.

Which was why I was going to see Ellie. While she was *his* sister, she was also *my* best friend and I knew where her loyalties lay—with me. I needed my best friend's advice and maybe a hug along with it.

Pulling onto the driveway, I was relieved to see only Ellie's shit colored car there. I loved Melinda and Henry, but I didn't think I was ready to face them just yet. They'd be bound to want me to sort things with Carter, and that would be by us getting back together. Problem was, I had all sorts of worries about that.

"Hey," Ellie said as she opened the door to me. "What're you doing here? I thought you'd be working today."

"Decided to take a few days and leave Lilah in charge."

I followed her through to the kitchen where she immediately turned on the kettle and pulled out a packet of chamomile tea.

"You got any vodka instead?" I asked with a laugh.

"That bad, huh?" She pulled me into the hug I so needed. "My brother again?"

I considered her question for a few and then said, "Actually no. I'm over him being an idiot."

"So, what's wrong?"

"Nothing as such. I'm glad Mom and Dad know. And the idea of being a momma is growing on me." Instinctively my hands cradled my tiny bump and I felt a surge of something in my chest. I wasn't sure what it was, but it felt warm and comforting. "I guess it's just the thought of having to make choices that are a little more grown-up than which purse to buy."

"It's only natural to feel that way." Ellie gave me a sympathetic smile and pushed a mug of tea toward me. "We're getting older. All our lives are changing."

She glanced over at some drawings and her face pinked.

"What are they?" I asked, getting up from my seat at the breakfast bar, my interest immediately piqued.

Ellie cleared her throat and followed me to look down on what appeared to be architectural drawings of a house.

"Oh my God," I cried. "Are y'all moving? Don't you dare tell me your mom and dad are selling their place. What will I do without you here?"

Ellie laughed. "Calm down." She looked at me warily from under her lashes. "It's Hunter, he's having the barn converted to a living space."

"He's finally decided to do that. At last, you'll get some privacy." I leaned down to take a closer look. "I thought he was just converting the upstairs to an apartment. This is like a *real* house. And why do *you* have the plans?"

Ellie blushed again as she took a deep breath. "He decided a house would be better. Well, he and Jefferson decided. There'll still be an office." She pointed to a room on the plans. "See there, at the back of the house overlooking the stables. And here, well they're going to build a small bunkhouse. Jefferson just bought twenty more acres from Lyle Matthews and wants to expand the herd at The Big D again this year so is going to take on four more ranch hands. That means with him, Hunter and the Williams brothers, there'll be eight of them working there. They're going to add on to the stables too, seeing as they'll need more horses. Oh and —"

"Ellie," I interrupted around a giggle. "Why are you babbling and why are you as red as a beet?

Staring at me with wide eyes, she chewed on her lip before blurting out, "Hunter asked me to move in with him."

"Oh my God," I screeched. "It's quick, but it's amazing. I'm so happy for you." Pulling her into a hug, I felt my face ache my smile was so big. Something struck me and I pulled away to look at her. "You seem unsure. It is what you want isn't it?"

"Yes, more than anything." Her face lit up, settling my concerns. "I didn't want to make you feel bad, with everything going on with you and Carter, is all."

My heart clenched a little. My best friend was happy and in love and I was unhappy and in love.

"Am I being stupid?" I asked, the words barreling from my head to my mouth. "Pushing Carter away."

"Bronte, you have to do what's best for you. I can't tell you and neither can your folks or mine. No matter how sad for everyone, if you don't think it's right with Carter, then you have to do whatever is necessary."

"That's the problem," I sighed. "Everything with Carter is amazing, most of the time. You know he's not the same with me as he is with you. He's kind, he's thoughtful and he's real funny."

Ellie screwed up her face. "We talking about the same Carter? Six-one, dark auburn hair, head as big as a bison's?"

"Yes," I laughed. "Seriously, Ellie, he's as sweet as cotton candy really."

"I guess I'll take your word for it." She shrugged. "Personally, I think he's a dunderhead and that you need help, but that's just me. So, why are you pushing him away, if you think all those things about him?"

"You know why. Because aside from all those things he's also selfish at times and is basically a fifteen-year-old in a twenty-six-year old's body. You know just before I found out I was pregnant he suggested we go travelling for three months. Go to Europe or India."

"Well, that's not unusual. I can see why he'd suggest it."

"I agree, but when I told him that would be cool, you know what he said?"

Ellie shook her head.

"He said, 'Oh, wait, I have to castrate Missy Malloy's Shar Pei next week. Maybe we'll do it some other time.'."

Ellie laughed and shook her head. "He's such an idiot."

"And he's my baby daddy," I protested. "You see why I'm scared, right?"

An arm came around me and I was bundled into another hug with my best friend. Thank goodness I had her, she understood me better than anyone.

"Okay," I said after Ellie began to squeeze a little hard. "Explain to me why there are three bedrooms and a den on that plan, when there's only two of you going to be living there?"

***

Spending time with Ellie, listening to her plans for a future with Hunter made me feel much better. By the time we'd had two cups of tea and a huge piece of Melinda's cherry pie, I was feeling totally relaxed.

"He has to be thinking of asking you to marry him," I gasped as Ellie showed me some swatches of fabric for drapes in Hunter's new house. "He wouldn't have asked you to move in if he wasn't. If I know anything about Hunter, it's that he doesn't do things on a whim."

Ellie shrugged and gave me a small smile. "I don't know. I hope so, but who knows?"

We'd gone back to looking at decorating ideas on Pinterest when the door burst open and Carter and Melinda walked in. They were carrying bags of groceries and chatting but as soon as she saw me, Melinda almost dropped hers.

"Bronte, sweetheart. How are you?" She put the bags down and came over to pull me into a hug, almost as tight as her daughter's.

"I'm good thanks," I replied as she let me go.

"Hey, Lollipop." Carter's beautiful whisky-colored eyes shone as he looked at me over the top of the bags he had in his arms. "I was going to call you."

"Is Roderick okay?" I asked, anxiously.

"Yeah, he's good. That's what I was calling for." He also placed his bags down and took a step closer to me. "You can pick him up later. Lance just wants to watch him poop and pee one more time, then he's good to go."

Heaving a sigh of relief, I ran to Carter and flung my arms around him. "Thank you, so much."

"Hey," he said rubbing my back in soothing strokes. "No problem. It's my job but gotta admit I took extra care of him, seeing as he's yours."

Suddenly feeling a little conscious that we were still locked in each other's arms, I pulled away. Ellie and Melinda were watching us, but quickly looked away.

"So," Melinda said briskly. "You want to stay for dinner, honey? Carter is and one more makes no difference to me."

"Mom," Carter warned before I could answer. "What did I ask you not to do?"

Melinda rolled her eyes. "Interfere. And for your information, Mr. Smarty Pants, I wasn't going to." She turned to me and took my hand. "This is a huge thing you're going through, honey, and I just want you to know we're here for you and our grandbaby no matter what happens."

She glanced at Carter and then back to me and I knew it must have been hard for her. There were so many things she probably wanted to say.

"Thank you," I replied. "And we do all need to talk, I guess, but in a few days when I've got my head sorted? Oh, and I'd love to stay for dinner please."

Melinda smiled, kissed my cheek and then set about putting her groceries away with Ellie's help, gossiping about Jacob Crowne's split from his wife

Lydia as they did.

"You okay?" Carter asked, coming over to stand next to me.

"Yeah, I'm good. I slept well last night, although I'll probably be asleep by the time your mom serves dessert."

"When you're tired, you just let me know and I'll get you home." He shifted his feet and ran a hand through his hair, looking nervous as all get out. "You still want me to come to your doctor's appointment with you?"

"God yes." I nodded. "I'm kind of nervous, so it would be good to have you there."

Carter let out a huge exhale and smiled. "Excellent. So, after dinner if you're not too sleepy I can take you to get Roderick before I drop you home."

"It's fine, I have my car."

"Yeah, I know," he replied, his brow furrowing. "But I'd like to and then I'll bring you back tomorrow for your car.

I considered carefully what he was suggesting. Dinner with his family and then time alone while we went to pick up my cat. I guessed it wasn't a big deal, and I didn't think he would take it as a green light for us to get back together. When I looked up to his handsome face, with the high cheekbones and straight nose, I realized even if he did it wouldn't be such a bad thing. I'd never stopped loving Carter; I was just being protective of the little baby we'd made together. And that was something I had to hope he felt the same way about.

CHAPTER 10

Carter

My ass was killing me and there was more sweat pouring from me than if I'd been working out; I was not a happy bunny.

"How long is she gonna be?" I hissed to Bronte who was busy reading some baby magazine. "This chair is not made to be sat on for an hour, and do they not know how to use their AC?"

Grabbing a pamphlet from the small table in front of us, I began to fan myself with it. That earned a stare from Bronte.

"That's meant to be read," she hissed, grabbing it from me and throwing it back onto the table.

I glanced down to see it was about protecting your nipples when breastfeeding.

"I have teat ointment at the clinic," I offered, nodding at the literature.

"For what?" Bronte's head shot up from her reading.

"Sore teats." Picking up the pamphlet again, I waved it in front of her, taking the opportunity to duck my face into the breeze. "So, it figures you could use it on your nipples too."

"You want me to smother my nipples in the same ointment that all the farmers and ranchers in the area cover their animal's titties in?"

I shrugged. "Teats, nipples, they're all the same."

Bronte took a deep breath and shook her head. "I actually despair of you, I really do."

Shit, I couldn't do anything right as far as she was concerned, so decided to sit quietly until it was our turn. I watched the clock on the wall and found myself counting the seconds in my head.

"Is there any chance you could be quiet." A heavily pregnant woman with a bad dye job and swollen ankles kicked at my foot. "You're really annoying. We can see what the time is, and that the doctor is running late. You don't need to tell us."

I turned to her and frowned. "I wasn't doing or saying anything."

"I can hear you counting, and if I can't hear you counting, I can hear you breathing." The woman's nostrils flared as she reached up to snap her bra strap which had fallen down.

"I'm sorry," I replied. "I didn't realize I was counting aloud. Was I counting aloud, Lollipop?'

Bronte narrowed her eyes on the woman. "Does it matter if he was? He can't help being a mouth breather, he has adenoid problems."

Puzzled, I opened my mouth to ask her what she was talking about, but Bronte gave me a glare that warned me to keep quiet.

"You might," she said quietly. "And therefore, she shouldn't be so rude. But stop counting the seconds. She's right, it's annoying."

Pouting like a toddler, I flopped back into the uncomfortable seat and crossed my arms over my chest. The temptation to poke my tongue out at the pregnant woman was strong, but I valued my balls. I was getting used to the idea of being a dad and wanted the opportunity to father more kids in the future.

After another eleven minutes and twenty seconds – yep, I counted – the door from the consultation room opened and I was surprised to see Marie

O'Reilly followed by her dad, Declan. As he moved to the desk, taking out his wallet, my eyes went straight to Marie's stomach to see a definite bump.

"It wasn't me," I yelled as I jumped to my feet and almost knocked my chair over. "I've never touched her."

Declan swung around and as soon as he spotted me, his face went red with rage. He'd once thought I was fooling around with Marie and had made it very clear it wasn't something that he was happy with.

"I swear, Declan," I said directly looking in his eyes. "No matter what you think, I have never touched Marie, or even breathed on her. I swear."

"Oh my God." Bronte groaned beside me and pulled on my jacket. "Carter, sit down. He knows it isn't yours."

I looked down at her and laid a hand on her shoulder. "I swear, Lollipop. I haven't, I would never."

She took a deep breath, closed her eyes and I saw her lips move.

"What are you doing?" I asked.

"Counting to ten," she ground out, her blue eyes flashing open. "Now, look over to who is standing with Marie."

I swiveled my head and heaved out a sigh of relief when I saw Evan Wickerson with his arm around Marie.

"Really? When did you two...?" I pointed between their crotches and grinned.

"Well at least five months ago," Declan said moving closer to me, his features morphed into something a little too menacing for my liking.

I sat back down in my seat and grabbed Bronte's hand. "No Declan, you can't hurt me. I've done nothing wrong and I'm going to be a father soon."

My grip on Bronte tightened and she let out a little whimper.

"Sorry, Lollipop." I lessened my hold and moved my gaze back to Declan who was clutching his wallet like he was wringing out a wet cloth. Hoping to alleviate the tension I smiled at him. "Congratulations, Grandpa."

Bronte groaned and Declan made a strange noise.

"I'd be glad if you didn't spread this around," Declan said through gritted teeth, the Irish brogue of his father's homeland whispering at the edges of his accent. "Folks will know soon enough, but it's not something Marie wants spreading around; being an unmarried mother."

Before the words had even disappeared into the ether, I felt both mine and Bronte's hackles rise. She, however, was faster from the gate than I was.

"You do realize we're no longer in ninety-twenty-five, right? There's nothing wrong with being an unmarried mother, which I have to say is a derogatory term in itself." She took a quick breath but was on a roll. "Many women choose not to marry the father of their child, or children, but it doesn't mean they are lesser citizens because of that and frankly Mr. O'Reilly, I'm saddened by your attitude."

Shit, I loved that girl.

"Yeah, what she said," I added, pointing to Bronte.

Declan shifted uncomfortably and then without a word, turned back to the receptionist and flung his credit card down on the desk. The atmosphere was a little tense. Marie and Evan appeared to be as nervous as Declan was mad. A seething Bronte threw her magazine down onto the table and nudged me.

"Please can you go and ask how long Dr. Baskin will be."

I snorted out a laugh, just as I'd done the first time Bronte had told me the name of her OBGYN.

"*His* name is not Carole," she said without even looking at me, like she'd already said it a dozen times – which come to think of it she had.

Deciding it best not to say another word, I lifted my numb ass off the seat to go and check with the nurse on the desk. Before I'd even moved a step, the consulting room door opened again and a real handsome guy shouted, 'Bronte Jackson'.

I looked over my shoulder to see that Bronte was standing and putting her purse over her shoulder.

"That's the doc?" I asked. "Him. The guy that looks like that Somerhalder dude?"

"Yes, why?" Bronte smiled, not for my benefit of course, and moved past me.

"Bronte. Hi, I'm Dr. Baskin, please come through."

We both followed him into his consultation room where there was a nurse filling in some forms. When the doctor went over and spoke quietly to her, I moved alongside Bronte.

"He's so good looking he's hurting my damn eyes," I whispered. "Don't they have someone older and uglier to look up your vagina?"

Bronte didn't respond and before I had time to add anything else, Dr. Baskin turned back to us, his Hollywood smile glowing in our direction.

"Okay, Bronte, if you'd like to hop up on the bed, and Dad you can sit in the chair next to it." He winked at me and while I really wanted him to look like a dick doing it, even I had to admit he looked pretty cool. "Once you're up there, Bronte, if you'd like to roll your yoga pants and underwear down so Maggie can then cover you and put the gel on for the sonogram."

Bronte nodded and passed me her purse with a shaky hand.

"Hey, Lollipop," I said, looking her in the eye. "It's going to be fine. We're about to meet our baby."

She nodded, exhaled a shaky breath and got ready for our life changing moment.

***

"Please don't cry," Dr. Baskin soothed. "I know it's a big thing, but everything looks healthy and normal."

"I'm just so emotional. I never expected to feel like this."

"Carter, you want a tissue?" Bronte asked and turned to Nurse Maggie. "Do you have a tissue for him, please?"

Maggie pulled a couple of tissues from a box and passed them to me over the top of Bronte's bare and slightly rounded belly. The belly where our baby was cooking away nicely.

"And you're sure you can't tell us if it's a girl or a boy?" I asked, wiping my eyes.

Dr. Baskin laughed. "I'm sorry, Carter, but it's a little soon yet. At your next sonogram, if you want to know I'll be able to tell you."

Leaning over Bronte, I peered at the screen and screeched. "There look, Lollipop," I cried, poking her on the arm. "I'm sure I saw a dick. Did you not see it?"

"I assure you," Dr. Baskin laughed. "You have no way of telling at this stage."

"Nope, sorry, you're wrong. I definitely saw a dick. Lollipop, don't you see it?"

Bronte turned her head back to the screen and sighed.

"Oh yeah, I do," she replied. "And it's the same size as yours. Like father, like son."

"What?" I gasped. "That's not true and you know it. Take that back right now."

"I'm not going to lie in front of our baby," she said, grinning at me. "That's not the right way to start parenthood."

Dr. Baskin and Nurse Maggie both began to laugh, but I was not amused. "You've hurt my feelings now."

"Oh, stop being an idiot." She took some paper towel offered to her and began to wipe away the gel. "A tiny wiener isn't anything to be ashamed of."

"I do not have a tiny wiener," I said directly to the hot doctor and his nurse.

"He gets embarrassed." Bronte sighed. "I've told him though, it's not a problem."

All three of them burst out laughing as I narrowed my eyes on Bronte who held up her pinky finger and wiggled it. So fucking funny.

"Excuse me," I said, feeling more than a little sulky. "I need the bathroom."

I left to a chorus of laughter behind me and will admit, I slammed the door a little too hard.

After I'd been to the bathroom, I paid for Bronte's treatment and filled in some forms with my healthcare details for future visits. I'd just about finished when Bronte came out of the consulting room holding a list.

"What's that?" I asked, taking it from her.

"Just some vitamins I need to start taking. Do you mind if we go to the health store and pick them up?"

"No, not at all. We can even grab some lunch."

I was feeling hopeful that maybe seeing the baby together would help Bronte realize we were meant to be. When she smiled and nodded, my heart thudded a little harder in my chest.

"I'll just settle up," Bronte replied.

"No need. All done and healthcare will be set up ready for your next visit."

She stopped in her tracks and stared at me, her eyes softening.

"Carter, no. My dad gave me his credit card."

I shook my head. "That's my baby, so I pay. There was never any question about that. Although, that little stunt with the tiny dick almost had me changing my mind. It wasn't a nice thing to say."

She gave a cute giggle and slapped playfully at my arm. "I've told you, don't sweat it. Not everyone can have a large penis."

Growling, I took my phone from my pocket and zipped off a text. Immediately Bronte's phone rang out. "You'd better check that," I said, a smirk on my face.

She looked at me quizzically, pulled her phone from her purse and tapped at the screen. When she opened up the text and grinned, I knew she was beginning to thaw.

There's nothing like sending a dick pic to your girl to remind her how big you really were and exactly what she was missing.

CHAPTER 11

Bronte

When Ellie and I had walked into Café Au Lait, there may have been a little part of me that hoped Carter would be there. Sitting at his usual table with Hunter, pretending to be all super fit and healthy but choosing his usual all-day breakfast. He hadn't been of course, and now we were almost ready to leave.

"They've gone to check a couple of bulls out," Ellie said, nudging me with her elbow when my head went to the opening door for about the fifth time. "Went real early this morning."

"Who?" I asked, feigning disinterest.

Ellie smirked and took a sip of her coffee. "You really should just forgive him for impregnating you, you know."

"Who?"

"Oh okay," she replied with a tilt of her head. "Exactly how many contenders are there? I thought my brother was the only one."

"Oh, him." I stirred my straw around in my strawberry and blueberry smoothie, wishing I could have a cup of coffee like Ellie.

"Yep, him. So, are you going to make up, make up, never, never break up?" she sing-songed.

I rolled my eyes. "You idiot, and I don't know. Depends whether he sends me any more dick pics or not."

Ellie's eyes slammed shut and she gagged. "I don't want to even think about my brother's penis."

God damn it, I did. It'd been almost three weeks since I'd last seen his big, beautiful member – dick pic aside.

"Well on other news," I said, changing the subject and searching through my purse. "I have this."

I pulled out my sonogram picture and presented it to Ellie.

"Meet your new niece or nephew. I forgot I had it with me."

Ellie grabbed the picture from my hand and gasped, putting a hand to her mouth.

"Oh, my God." She looked at me with dewy eyes. "It's real and so damn adorable. I can't wait for them to arrive."

"Of course, it's real." I laughed and leaned forward to look at the picture with her. "And it's making me crave licorice and peaches in the middle of the night."

"Really?" Ellie's gaze didn't waver from the picture in her hand. "When can you find out if it's a boy or girl?"

"Not for a few weeks yet." My thoughts went back to Carter and his insistence on being able to see the baby's penis, and I couldn't help but giggle.

"What's so funny?" Ellie pulled out her phone and snapped a photograph of the sonogram.

"Oh, nothing."

She looked up at me and passed the picture back and I couldn't help but laugh out loud again.

"Liar. Tell me."

"Oh, just your brother. He was insistent he could see it was a boy."

Ellie peered closely at her phone screen. "Sorry, no I don't see it. If it's there it's tiny."

"Exactly what I said." I gave her a wicked grin. "Told him it was the same size as his though."

"No way." Ellie gasped and then let out a deep belly laugh. "That is *the* funniest thing ever. I wish I'd seen his face. I'm betting he pitched a fit over it."

"Oh, he did. That was what the dick pic was for."

Ellie's eyes scrunched together as she laughed harder. "Someone feels insecure."

"Yeah, well." I sighed. "He has no need. Your brother is more than adequate in the schlong department."

God the memories.

"Erm, Bronte, do you think maybe you could close your mouth." Ellie's forefinger went under my chin and pushed it up. "You even have drool."

My attention was then taken as the door opened, and along with a warm May breeze, in wandered the man who starred in my dreams *and* nightmares, in equal parts. The little flutter of wings in my belly wasn't surprising because that was what Carter always did to me. The way his hair hung messily in his eyes, how his jeans always hung from his slim hips and the freckles that dotted his nose and cheeks, all added to the big package of gorgeousness. He could be inappropriate, grumpy, selfish and mean to his sister, but with me, aside from our bickering he'd always been sweet and generous. Not to mention how damn good he was in the bedroom.

Our first time had been a little bit of a shock all around. He was *so* much bigger than I expected for starters, but the fact that he'd got me back to his apartment and what he could actually do with that beautiful dick of his was even more astounding.

"Good morning, gorgeous." Hunter reached our table and leaned down to kiss Ellie's neck.

"Hey, you." Ellie was all starry eyed as she pulled him closer to whisper in his ear.

"Hi Lollipop. How you feeling?" Carter bent to kiss my cheek and when his fingers whispered over my belly, my heart fluttered.

"I'm good, thanks. We're good," I added, bringing a smile to his face.

"Did you manage to source the rest of the vitamins from your list?" he asked, picking up a strand of my hair and twirling it around his finger.

Although we weren't together, the intimacy of it made my breath hitch and wish that I weren't such an insecure idiot.

"There's a store at the mall which has them," I replied, trying to ignore his touch.

"Want me to go get them for you?"

I shook my head. "Ellie and I are going shopping after we've finished here."

Hunter's head popped up from nuzzling Ellie's neck. "Oh, you know what we need, baby. We're running out."

Carter's head whipped around to face him. "No," he snapped. "Don't say another fucking word. I do not want to know what you need. She's my damn sister."

"I might have been going to say condoms," Hunter protested with a grin.

Carter pointed at Ellie. "*She* takes the contraceptive pill and I know *you* got tested just after you started dating so you didn't have to use rubbers. So, whatever it is you're running out of, I do not want to know about."

Ellie gasped. "How do you know I take the pill?"

"I needed to borrow something from you." Carter shrugged.

"They're in my underwear drawer."

Carter shrugged again as if there was nothing at all wrong with snooping through his sister's panties.

"Anyway," I said, hoping to avert World War three. "We should get going."

The door opened again and Jimmy Foster, Dayton Valley Fire Chief swaggered in. He was tall, dark and handsome and since Hunter was off the market, had become Dayton Valley's most sought after single guy. He was a few years older than us but still went to the same parties and hung around Stars & Stripes every weekend. Still acting like he was twenty-two and carefree, instead of thirty-one and in charge of the town's fire safety.

"Jimmy," Carter greeted him. "No fires to put out?"

Watching him I saw Carter's shoulders tense. I'd got drunk one night and shared with him that Jimmy and I'd had a thing once. It had lasted all of one hundred and ninety-five minutes, but it'd still happened.

"Maybe Bronte still has a fire in her belly for me," Jimmy said, winking at me.

Ellie hissed. "He did not just say that?"

Jimmy laughed and turned to her. "Looking pretty today, Ellie."

Hunter took a step toward him, practically breathing steam through his nostrils but Jimmy held up a hand and laughed.

"Just messing with you." He turned to me. "So, the rumors true, Bronte? You're really having a kid with Carter?"

"Yes, it's true," I replied a little tightly, wishing he'd leave before he wound Hunter or Carter up any further.

"Well," he replied with a sigh. "That's a damn shame. I was hoping we could revisit the hot tub again. You remember that night, right?"

"I'd hardly call it a night, Jimmy," I replied, pushing my smoothie to one side. "And it's not something I'd really want to do again."

"Ah c'mon, Bronte, you know we had a great time." Jimmy smirked and glanced at Carter. "At least you sounded like you were having a good time."

"Hey now," Carter growled out. "That's my pregnant girlfriend you're disrespecting there."

He bunched his hands into fists and made a move toward our wonderful Fire Chief.

"It's a little joke is all." Jimmy placed a hand on Carter's shoulder and squeezed it. "You're just sore that you're getting sloppy seconds."

Carter's fist went out and Jimmy's expression was more scared than a cat at a dog pound.

"Carter no," I cried when he pulled his arm back for punch number two.

He paused, and turned to me, his face red with anger. "He disrespected you, Lollipop and that's not acceptable."

He turned away from me to finish what he'd started, but Jimmy had taken advantage of him being distracted and had started to move away.

"You're crazy," Jimmy cried, backing off and cradling his jaw. "I could have you arrested for attacking me. I'm the damn Fire Chief."

"He hardly attacked you," Hunter scoffed. "He barely even touched you.

Everyone knows Carter can't punch for shit."

"Take that back you dick."

"I'd have put him on his ass." Hunter shrugged. "Just saying, buddy."

"You know what," Jimmy said, holding his hands up in surrender. "She wasn't worth it anyway."

Without hesitation, I stood up, pushed Carter out of the way and threw my strawberry and blueberry smoothie all over Dayton Valley's Fire Chief.

Ellie and Hunter gasped while my beautiful, auburn-haired hunk, jumped up and down, punched the air and whooped with joy.

"Go, Lollipop," he cried. "That's my girl."

I beamed at him and felt my heart miss a beat, because deep down I knew he was right —I was his girl.

CHAPTER 12

Carter

"Bassinet, diapers, mobile." I ticked off the things on my list that I wanted to get for the baby. "Soothers."

It was pretty long, but I didn't care. I was going to make sure Lollipop didn't have to worry about a thing. Obviously, the stroller was on the list too, but I figured I should let her pick that. According to my mom, women could be real particular about the stroller they pushed their baby around in.

"Okay, let's do this."

Unbuckling my belt, I looked up at the Jackson house, wondering what reception I'd receive. The last few days Bronte and I had been getting along well. Dinner at Mom and Dad's had been great and when I'd dropped her home with Roderick, she'd even invited me in to help get him settled. Then there'd been the doctor's appointment and she didn't go crazy over me sending her a picture of my dick. Yesterday, after what had happened in the café, she'd even texted me to thank me for having her back with Jimmy Foster – fucking douche. So, I was hopeful today's visit would go smoothly; you just never knew with Lollipop and her hormones.

"Carter," Darcy greeted me cheerily when she opened the door. "Bronte's not here, honey but she'll be back soon. You want to come in and wait?"

Only taking a moment to consider my response I nodded. "That'd be great, thanks, Darcy."

It was good to see her smiling and I knew why when I went into the living room and Jim was in there reading the newspaper. It looked like things were progressing well with them.

"Hey, Jim."

He looked up and gave me the briefest hint of a smile. "Carter."

Okay, so maybe he was still pissed at me for getting his daughter pregnant.

"You want a drink, honey?" Darcy asked.

I was about to answer when my tooth started to throb. I'd had it all day and it was gradually getting worse. Feeling in my pocket for some painkillers I nodded.

"Water would be great please, but not too cold." I pointed at my mouth. "Toothache."

"Oh no. You got a dental appointment to get it sorted?" Darcy's brow furrowed as she rubbed my arm.

"Yeah, Tuesday. I can cope until then." I showed her the painkillers.

She gave me a sympathetic nod and then turned to her husband. "Jim, you staying for a drink?"

He folded his newspaper and gave her a smile. "Thought I might stay for dinner, if that's okay."

The way Darcy's face lit up, I guessed it was more than okay.

"Want to have a quick word with Carter too."

My stomach rolled at the thought. It wasn't that I was scared of Jim, more that I respected him. The thought he was disappointed in me didn't sit well and worried me more than him ripping me a new one.

Darcy gave me a comforting pat on the arm and left Jim and I alone.

"So," I said with a grimace. "I guess this is where you punch me, right?"

Jim raised his brows and pointed to the couch. "There'll be no punches thrown in this house. Now, sit."

Carefully lowering myself onto the couch, I kept my gaze on him, just in case he changed his mind.

"I've known you all your life," Jim said resting his hands on the arms of his chair. "You're a good boy and maybe I'd always hoped you and Bronte would eventually see each other for the good people you both are. All that fighting and arguing since Bronte could first talk was a little much at times, but Darcy always said it was foreplay to a great love."

I grinned and wanted to high-five his wife. "She wasn't wrong."

"You being apart doesn't actually back that up though, does it, buddy?"

"Not my choice, Jim."

"I know, I know." He nodded slowly. "But, got to wonder why she's pushed you away."

My shoulders slumped as I thought about how Bronte saw me. It was disappointing that she didn't think I was committed to her and the baby, that I wasn't up to the job. Admittedly before her I'd been a player, going from girl to girl and only caring about how I'd spend my paycheck at the end of each month. Then my Lollipop made my heart flip inside out. It might only have started out as one night of sex, but I'd quickly realized that one night wouldn't be enough. She changed me.

"She's worried I'm not in this for the long haul, Jim. But I am." I took a deep breath and looked him straight in the eyes. "I swear to God. Her, the baby, they're all I want. I'm ready for this. It's what I want."

Jim leaned forward and rested his forearms on his knees, his blond hair was greying at the temples, but his blue eyes, a mirror image of Bronte's, were bright and youthful. The stress of his relationship had taken its toll over the last few months, we'd all seen it, but watching him now it was clear that he was in a better place.

"That's good to hear, Carter," he replied. "Words don't mean anything though. It's actions that prove you're telling the truth. Thing is, son, you need to make sure you get that balance right. I thought buying Darcy anything she wanted or needed and just saying I love you was enough. As you know, it wasn't, and we ended up having problems. Her defense mechanism was to distance herself from me because she thought I didn't want her any longer. And actually, I thought she didn't need anything from me, except money." He sighed heavily and glanced at a picture of them on their wedding day. "We should have talked. I should have talked. I should have told her that I loved her how she was. I should have showed her instead of just writing a check. I should've supported her more with her mom. Betsy going into the home broke Darcy and I just let her deal with it alone, because I thought she could."

"But you're getting back on track, right?" I asked hopefully, not being able to stand the thought that they may crumble and never rebuild.

Jim nodded and smiled. "Yep, we are. I'm still staying at the apartment, for now, but it's great to be getting to know each other again. Starting afresh if you like."

I breathed out a sigh of relief. "Good, that's real good."

"Yeah, it is, but I don't want that for any of my kids. I want them all to know how hard it is to keep a relationship going and to be sure that they and their partner always make the effort." He sat back in his chair and ran a hand through his thick hair. "Maybe, it's our fault that Bronte is second guessing you and her and I'm sorry for that. You're a good man and I believe you when you say she and the baby are what you want."

"They really are, Jim."

He nodded. "Okay. So, you need to prove that you have the staying power to her. That you'll be the guy who always makes an effort with her, even thirty years down the line."

"I will, I swear." And I meant it. "A life without Bronte isn't something I even want to contemplate – now or in thirty years. I know it sneaked up on both of us after a lifetime of fighting, but now I can't picture my life any other way. Honestly, Jim, I love your daughter. I know I'll always love your daughter and I'll do whatever I can to always show her that."

Jim smacked the arm of his chair. "Okay then. I guess you have some work to do."

"Yes sir, I do." I pulled the shopping list from my pocket. "I came to talk to Bronte about maybe going shopping for all this. You think she'll go for it?"

Jim leaned forward, took the list from me and read it.

"That's a pretty long list," he said with a whistle. "And you know me and Darce will help out."

"No need. I'm good for it."

As he handed the piece of paper back to me, my mobile shrilled in my pocket and Darcy came into the room with a glass of water.

"Here you go, honey," she said, placing it on the coffee table as I pulled my phone from my pocket.

"Thanks, Darcy." I smiled up at her and then read the message. "Oh shit, sorry. I need to go. A horse has been caught in an RTA on the Middleton Ridge road."

Jim stood at the same time as I did. "Damn that's gotta be bad."

"Oh no," Darcy gasped. "I hope it's okay."

"Thanks for the chat, Jim," I said and moved for the door. "Will you tell Bronte that I called on her."

"Yes, sure, son. Now go and drive safe."

As I drove my car away from the house, I heaved a sigh of relief. Even though I was about to go and experience something pretty awful, it could never be as scary as facing Jim Jackson about his pregnant daughter.

CHAPTER 13

Bronte

"Hey, honey," Mom said as I walked through the door. "You just missed Carter."

My heart skipped a beat. "Carter was here? He didn't wait?"

"Had to go to an RTA," Dad answered as he came into the living room and kissed my head. "A horse is involved."

"Oh my God," I gasped. "I hope it's going to be okay." My heart lurched at the thought of Carter dealing with an injured horse in what might be a dangerous situation. "He'll be okay, right?"

"The horse or Carter?" Dad asked with a wry smile. "I'm pretty sure both will be fine. Carter's a great vet and the highway patrol will make sure he's perfectly safe."

Chewing on my bottom lip, I stared out of the window to my car.

"No, sweetheart," Dad said, running a hand down my hair. "Don't even think about it."

"I-I wasn't."

Mom laughed. "You can't fool us." She pulled me down onto the couch with her. "Honey, why are you doing this to yourself? You obviously love him."

Dad sat down on his chair, at least I supposed it was still his chair seeing as he didn't live with us any longer. Which was another thing, why *was* he at the house? I knew he'd called in for lunch with Mom, but it was way past that.

"I know you want him to be sure, sweetheart." Dad's eyes were full of concern as he looked between me and Mom. "And I've spoken to him and am pretty sure he's all in."

"You spoke to him?" My eyes widened as worry pulled at me. "You didn't hit him, did you?"

"No," Dad said around a laugh. "Of course, I didn't. We had a good talk."

"He's telling the truth, honey." Mom gave my hand a squeeze. "They just talked, and Carter was all in one piece when he left here a half hour ago."

"So, what did you talk about?" I asked.

Dad grinned. "What do you think? No need to worry though," he said, holding up a hand. "It was all perfectly amicable. I got to say sweetheart, I do believe he loves you and is committed to you and the baby."

"Dad's right," Mom added. "Maybe you should both talk."

Inhaling deeply, I flopped back against the many throw cushions Mom insisted on having on the couch.

"What is it?" Dad asked, leaning forward in his chair. "What's holding you back? Is it me and Mom?"

"Jim!"

"Darce no." Dad held his hand up to stop her. "We have to accept that our problems are going to impact the kids. It's bound to make them cautious."

Mom turned to me. "Is that true?"

I nodded slowly. "I guess so. I mean if you and Dad can't make it, what chance in hell do I have with Carter. The man's an interminable teenager. How the hell is he going to bring a child up?"

"Well firstly," Dad said, raising his brows. "Your Mom and me, well we're fine." He glanced at Mom, whose eyes were shining with love for him. "Well at least I think we will be. We just lost our way a little. But you know all the reasons why. We told all of you everything after our counselling sessions, so please don't let our mistakes color your future, sweetheart. No one wants you to be with someone you don't love, or want to be with, but I don't think that's the case with you and Carter. You should give it a go with him. And if it doesn't work out, you and the baby will always have a home here, with me and your mom."

I grinned and looked between my parents who were both smiling. "So, you're coming back home?" I asked tentatively.

Mom inhaled sharply as Dad paused to look up at the ceiling. It felt like time stopped for the few seconds it took him to reply.

Finally, he said, "Yes, if your mom will have me, but maybe not for a few weeks."

I looked over at Mom finding tears in her eyes. She'd missed him so much, but she knew him staying away for a little while was the best thing for them.

"Okay," she said breezily and pushed up from the couch. "I'm going to get dinner started. Dad is staying."

Dad cleared his throat and gave Mom a playful smile which made my heart skip a beat. They really were getting there and I hadn't realized how much I'd needed to hear it. The happiness it brought was the best feeling. Maybe Dad was right, maybe I should give Carter a chance.

"Do I have time for a shower?" I asked Mom.

"Sure honey. Austen isn't home from football practice yet anyway."

As I got up from the couch, a car pulled up on to the driveway. "Who's this?" I asked looking out the window.

"I don't recognize the car," Mom said, joining me at the window. "Do you, Jim?"

"Nope. Don't know anyone with a red sedan."

"Oh my God," Mom cried, rushing from the room. "It's Shaw."

My brother Shaw was at Harvard and wasn't due home for Spring Break for another week.

"What's he doing here?" I turned to Dad and saw he looked worried.

"No idea, sweetheart. But I guess we're about to find out."

We heard Mom open the front door and then squeal with joy that her baby was home. Before we had time to join them, she was dragging him into the living room.

Shaw looked tired with dark circles around his eyes, his blond hair was a little longer than he usually wore it and he looked thinner. I looked over to Dad and knew he'd noticed to; his mouth thinning into a line and his eyes narrowed on my brother.

"Hey, son. What's wrong?" he asked.

"Is something wrong?" Mom looked at Dad. She appeared to be clueless that Shaw looking a mess and being home a week early meant that of course there was something wrong.

My brother took a deep breath and rubbed at his forehead with his fingertips, his shoulders moving slowly up and down as the three of us watched him.

"Shaw, son, what is it?" Dad pressed.

"I don't know… Dad, I…"

Mom took his hand in hers and pulled on it. "Shaw, honey, what's wrong? What's happened?"

He looked conflicted as he looked between Mom and Dad, anguish in his eyes.

"Shaw, tell us," Dad insisted.

"I'm sorry but I got suspended."

"From Harvard?" I cried. "Oh my God, Shaw. What did you do?"

Looking at him carefully, his appearance told me there was only one thing it could be.

"You damn idiot," I hissed. "You've been caught doing drugs, haven't you?"

Shaw took a step back and murderous eyes stared at me. "What the hell, Bronte? I wouldn't do drugs; don't you know me?"

"Well, you look a mess," I protested, throwing my hands into the air.

"Well, that's because I've been travelling for almost eight hours. Not to mention putting in an all-night study session last night, seeing as I won't be around to hand in a paper next week."

"Well, you look like a meth-head," I protested.

"Hey, hey, hey," Dad said. "Just calm down the both of you. Son, tell us what got you suspended."

"Oh Shaw," Mom groaned. "I can't believe this. You worked so hard to get into that school. Do you know how privileged you are to be there? You could have been studying law there in a couple of years."

Shaw turned to Mom. "Of course, I do. I know exactly how many hours I put in to get there, you don't need to tell me."

"Hey, don't speak to your mom like that," Dad said. "Show her some respect."

Shaw looked suitably reprimanded and leaned to kiss Mom's cheek. "I'm sorry. I'm just so damn pissed about it all."

"So, tell us what the hell happened." Dad put his hand on Shaw's shoulder and gave it a squeeze.

"You're not going to like it."

"Shaw," Mom cried. "Just tell us."

He dropped his head. "My girlfriend, Monique, well, she's pregnant."

My mouth dropped open as Dad made a noise like he was being strangled.

"How the hell… you can't be serious," Dad groaned. "Two grandkids. What the hell?"

"Actually, no," Shaw replied, his tone low. "It seems she's been sleeping with our history Professor and he got her pregnant."

"Oh, my goodness, honey you must be devastated." Mom pulled him into her arms and kissed his cheek.

He maneuvered himself free and smiled at me. "No offence to you sis, but it's actually a relief. Kids are not on my schedule for a while."

My hands went to my belly and it hit me that I couldn't imagine babies *not* being in my schedule, particularly the baby already growing inside of me.

"The baby is the professor's then?" Dad asked. Shaw moved to stand in front of the fireplace, turned to face us and nodded. "And that got you suspended why?"

Shaw's face colored up and he cleared his throat. "I kinda punched him," he said quietly.

"*Shaw.*" Mom rolled her eyes. "Please tell me you didn't."

"I think he did, Mom." I began to laugh and high-fived my brother. "Good for you."

Shaw grinned back at me. "Put him right on his ass."

"You do know that this is your future you might have messed up, don't you?" Dad ran a hand through his hair and paced up and down. "What length of time are we talking? Have they said whether it'll affect you taking your law degree? Will they note it on your transcripts? Have they said? Did you ask?"

"Yes, Dad, I asked all of those questions. It won't affect my chances of Harvard Law if I get my undergrad degree and a good LSAT score. They've also agreed to keep it from my transcripts as long as I don't do anything like it again. Although," Shaw said with a sigh. "It's kinda soured my view of the place."

"You're not dropping out, son," Dad growled.

"No, I don't want to. I've worked too hard." Shaw blew out a breath. "But I am thinking of applying to Baylor, or Texas Tech—I can do a clinical program with them, and I kinda like the idea of that."

Mom's face shadowed with worry, and when I glanced at Dad, he looked the same. Shaw had worked real hard at high school because Harvard had always been his goal. He must have been feeling bad about everything to consider transferring after his undergrad studies.

"But you can stay and apply to HL if you want to?" Dad scrubbed a hand over his chin as he contemplated everything.

"Yeah, I can," Shaw replied.

"Did you get it in writing?" I asked. "Because they could say that now, but…"

"I go back after Spring Break and I got the Dean's word," he replied with a smirk. "They don't want the scandal of one of their professor's getting a student pregnant."

Mom laughed. "Like that's a scandal. I knew three girls at college who got pregnant by professors—one actually had the Faculty Dean's baby."

"Yeah, well, Mom," Shaw said. "This professor has four kids and is married to the *actual* Dean. The Dean who happens to be about to star in a reality TV show about running an Ivy League college."

"Really?" I gasped. "When does that start? Carter and I love reality TV shows. Oh, my goodness, I need to make sure we watch that."

"Bronte, sweetheart," Dad growled. "You think we could focus on the fact that your brother just got suspended from Harvard. And, while we are talking about all of this, who the hell does that car belong to? Don't tell me you stole the damn professor's vehicle as well as punching him."

"Shit, Dad, no," Shaw protested. "It's a rental from the airport. I figured it was better to get here and then tell you what happened."

"Shame." I peered around Dad to look through the window. "Nice set of wheels."

"Cool eh," Shaw responded. "Drives like a dream."

"Hey." Dad clapped his hands together. "I said, focus." He turned to Shaw. "And you're sure that this isn't going to come back on you after your suspension?"

"Yes, Dad. Dean Roberts doesn't want the scandal. As well as the show she doesn't want it affecting her sideline."

"What sideline?" Dad asked, putting fisted hands to his hips.

"She does a lot of mentoring and mock trialing with some of the big law firms and it earns her a whole lot of money. So, if it's on my transcripts, any law firm I try and get a job with will want to know the details. She's worried they'll spread it around, or even stop hiring her. Plus, what TV station wants their star caught up in scandal?"

"Oh, they'd love it," I offered enthusiastically. "I mean look how much airtime the Kardashians get when Kanye pitches a fit about something."

Dad gave me a withering look and sighed heavily. "Damn it, Shaw."

"I know and I'm sorry, but he deserved it. I liked her you know." He exhaled slowly and sadness shadowed his eyes. "Thought she might have been the one."

My heart sank for him. "Oh, Shaw, that's so sad."

He shrugged. "At least I know now she's a cheater and not when we've been married for a couple of years." He turned to me and winked. "You're lucky you found a good guy like Carter. He'll never let you down."

"But your sister broke up with Carter," Mom said with a sigh. "Don't forget that."

"That's only temporary. Right, Bronte?" Before I had time to reply, he turned to Mom. "Anyway, I'm starved. What's for dinner?"

As Shaw left for the kitchen, closely followed by Mom and Dad, I thought about his words. He was right, I was lucky to have found Carter even if he did drive me crazy from time to time.

So, I was decided I was going to get a good night's sleep and then tomorrow I was going to see Carter and tell him I wanted him back. I just hoped he still wanted me.

CHAPTER 14

Carter

When Delphine placed the plate of pancakes and bacon in front of me, I wasn't even sure I had the energy to eat them. Problem was my stomach was growling like a bear who'd just woken up from hibernation.

"Oh honey, you look exhausted," Delphine said, giving me a sympathetic smile. "Long night?"

"Yeah," I said around a yawn. "There was an RTA involving an SUV and a horse trailer. The horse was pretty messed up."

"Oh no." She clutched her hands to her chest, her smile disappearing. "Did you manage to save it?"

"So far so good. Chase Cameron the equine vet was treating a racehorse in Saratoga, but he arrived back a couple of hours ago. He's with him now, so fingers crossed."

"That's great, honey." Delphine gave my shoulder a squeeze. "You eat up and then go home and sleep."

Nodding, I popped a pain killer for my damned toothache and swallowed it down with a gulp of milk.

"They look great, Delphine."

She left me to go serve a group of girls that had come in for coffee on their way to the high school. Ten minutes later, I was slowly getting through my pancakes. Slowly because every couple of minutes I felt my eyes closing. Lack of sleep and painkillers for my toothache were killing me.

"Carter, you okay?" It was Nancy Andrews, my neighbor.

She was a teacher's aide at the Kindergarten and had no family to speak of after her folks died in a fire while on vacation a few years back. "You look awful," she said.

Prizing my eyes open, I looked up at her. "Jus' exhausted. Been up all night with a horse."

She bent down to look me closer in the eyes and frowned. "Have you taken something?"

"Jus ma pain killers for ma tooth." I could barely open my mouth to speak, everything came out slurred.

"Let me see them," she said quietly.

So quiet and soft, like a sweet, sweet, lullaby.

"Carter, show me what you've taken." Nancy shook my shoulder and gave my face a little pat.

Reaching into my pocket, I felt my head loll, like it was just too heavy for me to keep it upright.

"There ya go."

I slapped a pill bottle onto the table and watched through half-closed eyes as Nancy picked it up and read the label.

"Carter, how many have you taken?"

"W-wha?" I tried to take it from her, but missed my aim, landing my hand onto the table. "Shit. I don't think I can see."

"God," she groaned. "Okay, you sit tight while I call Doc Browning."

"Nah," I replied, waving her away. "I'll jus' sleep here."

"Carter, these are Extra Strength Tylenol," she said and put the bottle on the table. "How many have you had?"

There was an edge to her voice, like she was worried. I had no idea why and didn't care. I just wanted to sleep.

"I dunno. I need to think about tha..."

"Everything okay here?" It was Delphine's voice, but I couldn't see her. I couldn't keep my eyes open.

"He's taken Extra Strength Tylenol, but I don't know how many," Nancy said, her voice sounding far away.

"Carter, honey, can you tell us how many pills you took?" Delphine asked, shaking my shoulder.

"He doesn't know," Nancy replied. "You think I should call Doc Browning?"

"No, no, no, no," I said. "I know how many I took—six. Oh," I added holding up a hand. "I took three Advil PM as well."

"Oh my goodness," Delphine exclaimed. "Since when?"

"Since I wen' see my Lollipop las' night." I smiled thinking of her. "Imma gonna dream about her now."

"Carter, I think we should get you home," Nancy replied. "I'll take him. My class is on a field trip with Mrs. Baker and the Principal, so I have the morning off."

"You sure, Nancy?" Delphine asked.

"Carter, can you stand?"

I nodded and pushed up out of my seat. "Hey, I'm fine." My eyes opened and I straightened up, feeling a little burst of energy. "No nee' to come with."

Nancy shook her head. "No, I think I'll make sure you get home okay. Delphine, is his truck okay parked outside for now?"

"Sure. You want me to ask Garth to help you?"

"I'm fine," I replied, waving them away. "It's a five-minute drive home."

"No way, mister." Nancy threw her purse over her shoulder and took my arm. "I'll drive you."

"I nee' to pay," I protested, feeling sleepy again.

"Don't you worry, honey," Delphine replied, opening up the café door. "It's a few pancakes is all. You get home and get some rest and make sure you get that tooth looked at."

I saluted her and smiled. "Yes, ma'am."

"Come on," Nancy said. "Let's get you to bed."

Fifteen minutes later, after some pulling and pushing, Nancy finally had me leaning against the wall while she opened up my apartment. I'd got even sleepier and as I was on the third floor, I think she was pretty damn grateful the elevator wasn't having an off day. We lived in the same block, with Nancy just across the hallway, so when she got the door open, she knew exactly where the bedroom was.

"Okay," she huffed. "Here you go."

She practically threw me onto my bed, but as she did, I forgot to let go and pulled her down with me. As soon as my body hit the comfy mattress, it knew it had to go into sleep mode. Nancy tried to move away but she was all warm and comfy and so I just held on, rested my head against her chest and fell fast asleep.

CHAPTER 15

Bronte

I took a deep breath and pushed open the stair door which led to Carter's third floor apartment. I'd made my mind up; I was going to tell him how much I loved him and how much I wanted us to be a family.

Shaw had been right, Carter, for all he could be a fool at times, wouldn't let me down. I knew that but the shock of finding out I was pregnant had kind of spooked me. It'd had me second guessing everything, most of all, Carter.

Approaching the door of his apartment I saw that it was slightly ajar and wondered why. I knew Carter was home because I'd spoken to Lance. He'd told me that after staying up all night with the injured horse, Carter was taking the day to catch up on some sleep.

"Carter, you there," I called, rapping a couple of times on the door.

I pushed inside, straight into the large, airy living space with its black leather sofa and huge Lazyboy recliner. I damn well hated that chair; it was big and ugly and reminded me of trying to get Carter to put down his damn PlayStation and show me some attention. Over the months we'd been together, I'd tried to gussy up the apartment a little with lamps, throw pillows, rugs and towels which actually matched the bathroom, but the stupid chair was a real blot on my otherwise homely landscape.

Looking around the room, I was surprised to see it was still fairly tidy. I'd expected to be faced with a Carter size level of mess and destruction, but maybe my nagging had finally sunk in.

Moving through the living area to the kitchen, which was separated by a slatted, wood partition, I couldn't help but smile. The sink was piled with dishes, even though there was a dishwasher and on top of the stove was a dirty pan with what looked like dried up, day old spaghetti sauce—okay, so maybe he wasn't totally converted to be clean and tidy.

"Carter, babe, are you here?" I called, walking down the hallway off the kitchen.

It led to the two bedrooms and bathroom and I guessed that was probably where I'd find him.

"Carter."

"*Shit.*"

The voice I heard wasn't Carter's and was a little too feminine to be that of a burglar—or maybe that was me being sexist.

"*Oh my God.*"

Whoever it was started to groan and pant heavily. My heart started to pump rapidly, and my throat felt as dry as the desert as the noise of my rushing blood and that of the moaning thudded loudly in my ears.

The bedroom door was ajar and when I peeped through my nightmare became reality. I was right, it was a woman and she was writhing around underneath Carter.

"Oh my God, how could you?" I cried, tears burning my eyes.

"*Bronte, no,*" she called.

I looked closer and was shocked to see Nancy Andrews' face peering at me over Carter's shoulder. Her face was crimson, and her hair was a mess as she clung onto his shoulders.

I gasped as the douche canoe who I'd thought I'd wanted to make a life with, nestled closer to her and wrapped his arms tighter around her. He was either totally oblivious that I was there or didn't give a shit at how many pieces my heart was shattering into.

"I-I hate you," I cried, turning to run, only hearing Nancy's voice resounding in my ears as I bolted the apartment block into the parking lot.

"What the hell is wrong?" My brother asked as I ran into him.

I'd given him a ride into town as he wanted to go to the bank while I visited with Carter, but he must have finished and been looking for me as he was walking toward Carter's apartment building.

"I-I can't say," I cried.

His arms came around me and held me tight against his chest as I sobbed and desperately tried to erase what I'd just seen from my memory.

"Sis, what is it?"

I gulped in the air my shoulders shuddering up and down. "C-C-Carter and N-N-Nancy."

When I let out a loud, shrieking cry, my brother pulled his head back and grimaced. "Shit, Bronte, that was loud."

"I'm heartbroken," I yelled. "What do you expect?"

Another loud sob pushed out of my mouth, but this time Shaw pulled me closer to him and tightened his arms.

"Tell me. What about Carter and Nancy?" he soothed, brushing a hand down my hair.

I shook my head, unable to say the words or articulate what I'd seen.

"Sis, I can't help you if you don't tell me," he whispered against my ear. Another sob and my brother's hand rubbed up and down my back. "Tell me."

"I went up there."

Shaw nodded. "Yeah, I know, so what happened? Did you argue?"

"No," I sobbed shaking my head. "He was in bed with Nancy Andrews."

Shaw held me away from his body and stared at me. "Say what?"

"Carter was in bed with Nancy when I got to his apartment. He didn't even look at me."

"What!" Shaw's eyes went wide and his nostrils flared as he looked down on me. *The father of your kid was in bed with another woman?*

My bottom lip jutted out as my chin quivered. "He was so into her he didn't even know I was there."

Shaw gasped. "What like literally 'in' her."

Images of Carter on top of his neighbor flashed through my mind, tearing another sob from my chest.

"He was actually having sex with her?"

"They had their clothes on," I said through my tears. "But it was obvious where it was going. He was writhing up and down on top of her, Shaw. He was snuggling her boobs."

Another round of weeping from me brought more soothing whispers from my brother as he hugged and rocked me from side to side. Finally, I stopped crying and pulled away from him.

"I can't believe it. He didn't even stop, Shaw."

Shaw's eyes were dark as he looked down on me. "Fucking dick. Well, he doesn't treat my sister like that." He turned me around and pushed me toward my car. "Get in the car."

"What?" My mouth dropped open as I watched him storm toward the entrance. "No, Shaw, leave it."

Running up to him, I grabbed hold of his hand, but he shook me off and pushed at the door.

"What the fuck is his code to get in?" he asked.

"No." I shook my head. "I'm not telling you. I don't want you to go up there."

"He doesn't hurt my sister and get away with it." Shaw growled and pulled his phone out of his pocket and began stabbing at the screen.

"Let's just go," I pleaded, in between sobs. "Please, Shaw."

"No, the little fucker is getting what's owed to him." He looked to the keypad on the door and started to punch numbers in. "Yes," he hissed as the door pushed open.

"How-?"

"Blake Lively's birthday. I Googled it," Shaw muttered. "He's nothing if not predictable."

As he pushed inside the building, the door almost whacked me in the face. I just managed to put out a hand and stop it before chasing after my brother.

He bounded up the stairs almost two at a time, with me trying to catch up to him.

"Shaw, no," I hissed as he banged on the front door that I'd only minutes earlier slammed shut.

"The little cock sucker is going to get a punch on his nose." Shaw thumped his closed fist against the door again. "Maples, get the fuck out here now."

The door didn't open, but I could hear muffled shouts from the other side.

"Is she fucking kidding?" Shaw asked. "She's shouting your name. Is Carter a damn kink or something?"

I listened carefully and Shaw was right, Nancy was shouting my name.

"He's gone crazy," I hissed. "Why is he making her call my name?"

Shaw's jaw tightened as he shook his head. "He's a damn sicko, that's why." He turned to face me. "Key, now."

I stared down at his open palm. "Nope. You'll do something stupid."

"I'll punch his damn lights out, that's what I'll do. Now give me the key, Bronte."

"Please don't punch him." I grabbed hold of his fist that was about to bang on the door again. "He thinks we're on a break."

Shaw's mouth dropped open and his eyes went wide. "What? Do I need to call you Rachel Green now?"

"No," I replied. "But I've been pushing him away and he must have just got pissed at waiting for me to wise up."

"Wise up to what?" Shaw demanded. "That he's an idiot with his brain in his dick."

When Nancy's voice shouted out for help, we both looked to the door.

"Is he forcing her?"

"No, Shaw, he wouldn't do that," I gasped and pulled out my keychain. "Here, go in but don't you dare punch him. If you do feel the need to hurt him just stay away from his hands and his face."

"I get the hands," Shaw said as he put the key in the lock. "He needs them for his job, but his face?"

I sighed and hated myself for thinking it. "He's too pretty."

As he pushed open the door, Shaw rolled his eyes. "Maples get the fuck out here now. I do not want to see your bare ass."

"Help me please."

"Help her," Shaw said storming toward the bedroom. "I'll throw her out naked if I have to."

"Shaw, no."

He held his hand up to silence me and continued toward what I'd started to consider our bedroom, even though I didn't live there. That thought hurt my heart seeing as it wasn't our room any longer. I paused as Shaw reached the open door and when he disappeared inside, I knew I couldn't avoid it any longer. As much as it would kill me, I had to know for certain that Carter had done something I'd always known he eventually would— to realize settling down wasn't for him.

Rushing after Shaw I followed him to the bedroom and barreled into the back of him.

"What's going on?"

I looked over Shaw's shoulder and inhaled sharply. Nancy was grunting and huffing, trying to push Carter off her. His deep auburn hair was all mussed up, his arms were wrapped around her like she was the comfiest pillow and he was snoring, sounding like a chainsaw.

"What the actual fuck?" Shaw moved forward and pointed at Nancy. "What the hell do you think you're doing? You do know he's having a baby with my sister, right?"

"Of course, I do. Now do you think you could get him off me?" Nancy gave Carter another shove and then blew her bangs from her eyes. "A hand would be nice instead of being rude to me."

The glare she gave my brother could easily have turned anyone to stone. It was full of spit and fire.

"*Rude*," Shaw exclaimed. "Me, be rude to you. The woman who has hopped into bed with my sister's baby daddy. Now, how the hell do you figure that out?"

"Hmm, Lollipop." Carter snuggled closer to Nancy and smacked his lips. "So comfy."

"He thinks that's me." I poked Shaw in the side. "Why would he think that?"

"Probably because she got him drunk and then enticed him into bed."

"I did not," Nancy cried alongside a grunt as she gave Carter another push. "I helped him home from the café. He's been up all night with a horse and taking painkillers for his toothache."

"Oh, so you drugged him." Shaw pointed an accusatory finger at her. "You really are a piece of work, lady."

"He still hasn't been to the dentist. He's had that damn cavity for months." I moved to the side of the bed and looked down at Nancy. "He took painkillers on an empty stomach, didn't he?"

"He was eating at the café, but I'm not sure how much he got down him seeing as he was falling asleep at the table. All I did was help him home, Bronte. He was so out of it I brought him in here and he fell on top of me, trapping me," Nancy explained and then grimaced. "He doesn't look as heavy as he actually feels."

"God, I know it," I replied with a smile. "When he falls asleep, he's literally a dead weight."

"You believe that?" Shaw asked incredulously. "That he fell on top of her. I suppose his dick just fell inside of you too, did it?"

Nancy inhaled slowly and blinked slowly. "You think you could tell your brother to… you know… go fuck himself."

"Me go fuck myself?" Shaw responded. "As opposed to you fucking my sister's boyfriend?"

"I didn't damn well fuck him," Nancy cried, attempting to throw her arms in the air. "I told you what happened and when he wakes up, Carter will tell you the exact same story."

"Oh of course he will." Shaw smirked. "Because he's going to tell any lie he can to make sure my sister doesn't dump his ass."

"Shaw," I snapped. "Just leave it. I believe her." I turned back to Nancy. "I'm sorry, my brother can be a dick at times."

"Yeah, well," she grumbled. "That'll be the trainee lawyer in him."

"And what's that supposed to mean?" Shaw asked, widening his stance and putting fisted hands to his hips.

"You're the brainbox, Shaw," Nancy spat back. "You work it out."

"Says the girl who was always the ass licker in high school," Shaw returned.

"Will you both quit it." I rolled my eyes and sighed heavily. "Help me get Carter off Nancy and then you can apologize to her for being rude."

Marching over to me, grumbling under his breath, Shaw put his hands under Carter's armpits and pulled him off Nancy. Throwing me a sarcastic smile, he unceremoniously dumped him onto the other side of the bed.

"Thank God." Nancy groaned and pushed off the bed, swiping the back of her hand over her forehead. "I thought I was going to die there."

She stood a few inches from me and gave me a small smile. "I'm sorry, Bronte, it really wasn't what *he* said." She flashed a warning glare at Shaw. "Carter really was dog tired. He told me he'd taken some Advil PMs on top of six painkillers."

"Six!" I exclaimed.

Nancy nodded. "Those mixed with the Advil, no sleep and a near empty stomach just knocked him clean out."

"It's fine, Nancy. I'm just sorry my brother is such a rude douche." I looked her up and down. "Are you okay?"

She rubbed her side. "Yeah, but he has real boney elbows."

I grinned. "I know, he gets me with them most nights."

"Are we finished with the sweet girly catch up?" Shaw ground out. "Any chance we can go home now?"

"I'm not going anywhere," I replied looking down at Carter who had upped his snoring a notch. "I want to check he's okay."

"Really?" Shaw asked.

"Yes, really."

"After what he did, with her?" He pointed at Nancy who was brushing her long dark hair back from face.

"I told you, it was nothing like that," Nancy replied looking at my brother like he was a big pile of horse manure she'd just stepped in. "Why are you such a dickbutt? Were you born like that or did you learn it at that fancy Ivy League college of yours?"

"Well, we all know you were born an uptight bitch."

"Shaw," I gasped. "Apologize now, god damnit."

What the hell was his problem with Nancy? I believed her, so why didn't he?

"Don't worry about it, Bronte." Nancy huffed out a breath. "Just make sure Carter gets that tooth checked out. Oh, and I forgot to bring his painkillers from the café, so you may need to get him some more."

I nodded and gave Nancy's arm a squeeze as she moved past me toward the door, shoulder barging Shaw on her way out.

I turned on him. "Well, you were rude."

"Yeah well, she deserves it. Been a bitch since high school and evidently hasn't changed since."

Carter groaned, rolled onto his back and then rubbed at his nose.

"He's waking up," I told Shaw, recognizing the tell. "You take my car and tell Mom I'll call her later."

"You can't be serious about staying with him?"

"Yes, Shaw I am. Weren't you the one who less than twenty-four hours ago was telling me what a good man he was?"

He rolled his eyes. "Yeah, before we found him in bed with Nancy Andrews. Which kind of makes me a shit judge of character, dontcha think?"

Exhaling heavily, I turned my gaze back to Carter who was most definitely waking up—he was scratching his balls.

"Just go home, Shaw."

Shaw looked to Carter and then back to me. "If I find out Nancy Andrews was lying, I'll chop those balls off and that baby you're carrying will be the last of his fucking bloodline."

"What's going on?" Carter asked, looking at me with only one eye open. "I wasn't dreaming, you're here, Lollipop."

Shaw opened his mouth, but I slapped my hand over it. "How're you feeling?"

He winced and put a hand to his cheek. "Still have a fucking toothache. That's what woke me." He patted the pockets of his jacket. "You seen my painkillers? I had them in the café."

"The café where you hooked up with Nancy Andrews," Shaw griped.

"Shaw," I snapped. "I told you to go home."

Carter pushed himself into a sitting position and scratched his cheek. "What the hell are you talking about?" he asked. "I remember eating pancakes and then Nancy offering to give me a ride home, but after that." He let out a loud yawn. "Don't remember much, except sleeping and dreaming about you Lollipop, except it wasn't a dream because you're here."

He gave me the most beautiful of sleepy smiles but then winced and flopped back against his pillows.

"Shaw, make yourself useful and go check for painkillers in the cabinet in the bathroom."

He began to grumble but when I pinched his side after Carter gave another groan of pain, he left the room.

"Shit, I really need to see the dentist," Carter said, clutching a hand to his face.

"Yeah, you do." He certainly didn't look like a guilty man, just a tired one wracked with pain.

He *was* fully clothed, and Nancy had been too. It did seem pretty unlikely anything had happened between them.

"Nancy may well have been telling the truth." Shaw shoved a bottle at me. "If these are the same as the ones he took with the Advil, there's no way he'd have managed to even think about getting his dick up, never mind actually getting it up."

I looked at the label and saw it was emblazoned with *Extra Strength Tylenol.*

"Are these the same as the ones you had in the café?" I showed them to Carter.

He grimaced and pulled in a breath. "Yes. I just need them until my dental appointment next week."

"Carter," I cried. "Why have you not been to the dentist? The number of pills you've taken along with the Advil and no sleep, no wonder you pretty much passed out."

I turned my gaze on Shaw, who shrugged. "Okay, so maybe Nancy was telling the truth. Look, I'm going to go."

"At last. And be careful in my car."

He shuddered and turned for the door. "Can't believe I have to drive that thing. It's fucking pink for starters."

"I hear you, Shaw," Carter said around a pained laugh. "I keep telling her to trade it in for something more suitable. A nice SUV that can handle the winters, but she won't listen to me."

I pushed a hand against Carter's shoulder, emptied two pills from the bottle and passed them and a bottle of water from next to the bed to him. "That's the last two you're getting. I'm going to call the dentist and get you an emergency appointment. You take them and get some more sleep. And *you*," I pointed at my brother, "go home and stop saying shit about my car."

Shaw sighed and with a wave of his hand left me alone with Carter.

"You know, Lollipop, I'd sleep much better if you got on here with me." He patted the mattress and I had to admit, it did look comfy.

I could have done with a little rest, but I knew if I got onto that bed with him, it would be so much more than taking a nap. It would probably be the start of us being an 'us' again. It would be me admitting that I trusted Carter with mine and the baby's heart. Yet how could I when I'd mistrusted him even though I should have known better.

"Sleep," I said with a sigh. "I'm going to call the dentist and then when you wake up, I'll make you some dinner."

Carter gave me a sad smile and nodded. "Okay. Sounds good to me."

Touching the edge of the comforter that I'd picked out, I sighed and left the room, wondering whether I'd ever come to my senses.

CHAPTER 16

Carter

Two days after having my cavity filled, I felt like a new man; as far as the pain was concerned anyway. Bronte was still being determinedly stubborn about us; despite the fact I was pretty sure she'd wavered when I'd asked her to get into bed with me. The little hitch of her breath was the tell.

Whenever she was turned on and close to rocking my world, she always did this thing where she breathed in and did a little gasp at the same time. Well, I'd heard it that day in my apartment, so the future didn't look completely bleak. I just needed a little more help.

"Hey, Aunt J," I called up to the front porch of the house as I slammed my truck door. "Where's that big ugly lug of a nephew of yours?"

"Oh hello, Carter, honey. How are you?"

The sweet little old lady was dressed in a yellow sundress with big pink roses on it and frills at the sleeves. On her feet were what looked like wooden clogs that I'd seen in books about Holland. Some might have been a little surprised by the attire but nothing Hunter's aunts wore or did shocked anyone in Dayton Valley.

"I'm great. How about you?"

As I walked toward her, I noticed a fat puppy at her feet chewing on a shoe.

"Who's this little guy?" Stooping down I rubbed its head, giving a quick look under its belly. "And it is a little guy."

Janice-Ann's face fell. "Really?" She turned and called over her shoulder, "Lynn-Ann, Primrose is a boy."

Janice-Ann's identical twin appeared in the doorway with a bowl of what looked like oatmeal and wearing the exact same dress as her sister but in pink with yellow roses.

"Are you sure?" she asked, looking crestfallen. "I'm sure you're mistaken."

"Carter said—"

"You can't believe a word that boy says," Lynn-Ann retorted moving forward and spotting me. "Oh hi, Carter, honey."

She wasn't even phased that she'd been caught out on calling me a liar.

"Tell her, Carter," Aunt J said.

I shrugged my shoulders and passed 'Primrose' to Aunt J. "She's most definitely he, I'm afraid." I indicated for her to lift the puppy up and showed her and wondered how the hell they'd missed it—although it was the twins we were talking about.

"Darn it," Aunt L hissed.

"I have my bag with me, you want me to check him out?"

Aunt J snuggled him to her chest. "Would you, honey? We'd be really grateful."

"No problem. I'll visit with Hunter and then call back to the house. That okay?"

The two sisters nodded in unison.

"Where'd you get him, anyway?" I asked.

"Pauly Jansen's dog had puppies and he was going to take them all to the pound," Aunt J explained. "We saw him at the gas station when we were there with Jefferson, so we decided we wanted one."

I smiled. "And I'm guessing you went on at Jefferson until he said yes. Am I right?"

They both grinned.

"Janice-Ann refused to come out of the rest room until Jefferson agreed."

"How many others were there?" I asked, giving him another scratch behind the ears.

"Three," Aunt L retorted.

"And what happened to the other two?" A thought came into my head. "Did Pauly take them to the pound?"

"No." I looked up to see Jefferson. "They're in my damn barn. And that is my shoe it's having for breakfast."

"He won't let them in the house. He made us pick one out," Aunt L pouted.

Jefferson rested his hands on his hips and looked down at the ground. "And didn't that take longer than a cow with a breach birth," he muttered.

"What are you going to do with the other two?" I asked, my idea taking shape.

"Why, you know someone who'll want one?" Jefferson asked, looking up at me with hope in his eyes.

"Well, there's nothing like owning a dog to tell a woman you're ready to be a dad, right?"

Jefferson took a step back and winced. "Carter, son, are you sure that's the right way to go about things. You know better than anyone how much work puppies are, and with a baby on the way…"

"I know." I shrugged. "Like I said, it proves a point."

Jefferson's eye roll didn't escape me, but I didn't care, I knew it was the right thing to do. There was nothing like a fluffy little animal to soften a girl's heart.

"I'm going to go pick one," I informed them.

"There's a boy and a girl," Jefferson informed me. "They're at the back of the barn in an old tack crate. Hunter is in there changing the oil on the truck."

"What're you ladies going to call your little guy now?" I asked, already deciding I was taking the boy.

Hunter's two aunts gave me identical frowns. "Primrose," they chorused in a tone that said I was stupid.

Jefferson shrugged and gave me a look as if to say, 'see what I'm up against'.

"Okay." I scratched my head and pointed toward the barn. "Once I've finished talking with Hunt I'll give them all a check over."

"Thanks, Carter." Jefferson slapped my back and leaned in close. "Maybe see your way to swapping this guy out with the little girl. I'm not sure I can be responsible for him having a dick and answering to Primrose."

Laughing, I nodded and walked away toward the barn to find my best buddy not with his head under the hood of the truck as I expected, but pacing up and down, mumbling to himself.

"Hey, what's going on?" I asked, my eyes searching for the crate.

Hunter barely glanced at me as he carried on wearing a path in the sawdust and hay on the floor.

"Hunter, buddy, what's going on? Your dad said you were changing the oil on the truck."

He looked over to me and scrubbed a hand down his face. "What do you want? I'm kinda of busy right now."

"Yeah, looks like it." Leaving him to stride, I went to the back of the barn where a big, old wooden crate was making little yapping noises. "Hey, there guys."

Inside were two more cute little puppies. One was all black and the other black and gold, just like 'Primrose'. At a quick glance you wouldn't have a clue what breed they were, but I knew Pauly's bitch, Sadie, was a Golden Retriever. As for the dad, it could have been a Coonhound by the length of the puppy's ears. They were handsome little fellas and I knew one would most definitely make Bronte all gooey inside. Picking each up in turn, I could see that Jefferson was seemingly better at gender spotting than his sisters. He was right, there was a boy and a girl.

"I'm taking the boy," I announced to Hunter, whether he was listening or not. "Gonna call him—"

"Do not say, Blake," Hunter snapped from behind me.

"Oh, so you are listening then?" I turned to see a real pale face. "What the hell is wrong with you? You sick or something?"

"No," he groaned and tugged at his hair.

"Well, you look sick," I offered as I picked up my new puppy. "Hey, Mani, how are you doing?"

"Mani?" Hunter asked.

"Yep," I replied without turning away from the cute hairy face in front of me. "He's Bronte's favorite member of The Stone Roses."

Hunter shrugged.

"British indie band?"

He shook his head. "No idea but if you've finished you can go. Like I said I have stuff to do."

"What the hell's crawled up your ass?" I placed Mani back with his sister and turned to my best friend. "I actually needed your advice but if you can't be bothered to help a friend, forget it."

"You know what, Carter, it isn't always about you. Sometimes other people have stuff going on too."

"What've you got going on?" I asked, raising a brow. "Apart from faking changing the oil on your truck."

"Just stuff." Hunter raised his brows and thrusting his hands into his pockets, nodded toward the door. "Now, you think you can go?"

Contemplating just doing as he asked, I eyed him up and down noticing his eyes were looking at everything except for me.

"What are you hiding from me?" I felt a thud in my chest remembering the last time I thought he'd kept something from me—that he'd kissed Bronte. He hadn't, but I'd still put him on his ass with one punch.

"I'm not hiding anything," he protested. "Just fuck off and leave me alone." He stalked toward me and when he pulled his hand from his pocket to take hold of my arm, a piece of paper glided to the floor.

"You dropped something."

As I bent to pick it up, Hunter was on me in a flash trying to snatch it from under my fingertips.

"Hey what is it?" I laughed. "What don't you want me to see?"

Snatching up the piece of paper, I pushed Hunter away from me, sending him stumbling backward.

"You fucker," he cried. "Don't you dare read that."

"You idiot. Don't you know that telling me not to read it is a surefire way to get me *to* read it."

Hunter's face crumpled with realization as I lifted the piece of paper and began to read it aloud.

"Ellie, my beautiful, sexy woman. You know how much I love you." I paused and looked over to Hunter who had his head in his hands. "I can't imagine a life without you, not ever. You're all I think about, the only person I want to give my heart to, so that's why I'm going to ask you…"

I scanned the rest of Hunter's scrawl and then my eyes almost popped out of my head.

"You're going to propose?"

"Yeah, and?" He turned away and stalked toward the barn door. "Just go, Carter. Give me the paper back and then fuck off and leave me alone."

"I can't believe you're doing this," I cried, shaking the piece of paper at him.

Hunt took a step back toward me, his hand outstretched. "That I'm going to propose?"

"Exactly that."

"You must have had some idea. You know I damn well love her to distraction; you give me enough shit about it. Plus, we've been together a couple of months—"

"Yeah, a couple of months," I yelled, throwing my arms into the air. "I've been with Lollipop for almost six and she's pregnant. It should be me proposing not you. You, selfish bastard."

Hunter leaned into my space. "Me selfish?"

"Yeah, you."

He shook his head. "Only you could spoil this for me when you know what she means to me."

"It's the order of things, Hunt." Looking down at the piece of paper I curled my lip. "You and your damn sexy words, it's all so easy for you. Whereas me, I impregnated my girl and she dumped my ass. I came here to ask you for advice on how to get her back, but you have to spoil it by being some fucking Casanova who just clicks his fingers and gets my damn sister to marry him."

"She hasn't said yes, yet. I haven't even asked her yet."

I threw my hands into the air. "But we all know she will. Who could deny the great and wonderful Hunter Delaney?"

"Why, you selfish prick."

The punch came before I even saw it. It wasn't hard, we were best friends after all, but it was enough to land me in the hay and sawdust.

"What was that for?" I yelled looking up at Hunt who was looming over me.

"For being a spoiled brat." He held his hand out to me. "Now, get up."

Taking his hand, I allowed Hunt to pull me to my feet and growled at him. "Dick."

"Well, takes one to know one," he muttered.

Brushing down my jeans I glared at him and when he stared back, still looking kind of sickly, I burst out laughing.

"So, you really want to spend the rest of your life with Ellie?" I asked.

Hunter nodded and a small grin appeared on his face. "Asked your dad's permission, got a ring and everything. So, yep, I want to spend the rest of my life with Ellie."

"And you called me a dick."

Hunter rolled his eyes and stooped to pick up his speech that I'd dropped on the floor. "Just don't pressure her," he said, folding it and pushing it into his back pocket. "Bronte. Give her space and she'll realize what she's missing."

Smiling over at him I nodded. "Thanks buddy. Appreciate it."

"Yeah well, another word of advice; *do not ever* mention again about calling your kid, your dog, or even the first goldfish you win at the town fair for that kid *Blake*. Not if you really want Bronte back and want to keep her."

I staggered backward. "What the hell... how could... you are so out of order."

Hunt sighed, turned and walked out of the door muttering something about me being the biggest douche on the planet.

"Well, Mani," I muttered, picking up Bronte's gift. "That was rude."

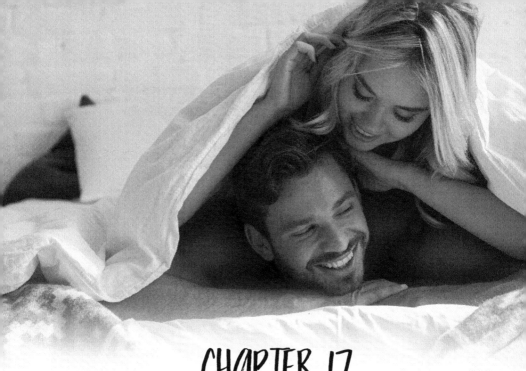

CHAPTER 17

Bronte

Pushing my shopping cart around the food market, my mind was constantly flitting to thoughts of Carter—moreover sex with Carter. It had been weeks since I'd been sexed to perfection by him and I was starting to feel withdrawal symptoms.

Hah, wrong choice of words because not withdrawing was what had me searching the shelves for canned peaches and licorice. At two a.m. that morning I'd almost been in tears because Mom only had canned pineapple in the cupboard, and let me tell you, it was a damn poor substitute.

Finally, finding myself in front of cans and cans of fruit, I stared at them in awe. There were three different kinds and two were on special. Pure bliss!

"Hey, Lollipop."

Whizzing round to face Carter, my heart did a little skip. God, he looked beautiful. His hair was mussed up and flopping in his eyes, and he was wearing jeans and a navy-blue tee which stretched across his chest pretty nicely.

"You not working today?" I asked inhaling and letting out a little gasp at the same time.

Carter grinned and the way his eyes twinkled I had a feeling that he knew something I didn't.

"Nope, not today. Lance and the new assistant are holding the fort. I've got some days owing so I'm taking a few of them."

"Doing anything nice?" He looked so damn good, and smelled amazing, it worried me that the something he knew that I didn't was another girl.

"Just chillin'."

His eyes darted to his cart so mine followed. Inside was a box of puppy pads and a chew toy.

"What are they for?" I pointed at the contents.

"A puppy, believe it or not." He gave a short laugh, the one I knew he gave when he thought he was in trouble. "Just for a client who has a puppy and can't afford much."

His gaze then darted to the left and I knew for definite he was lying to me and it left my insides feeling all mushy and my chest aching. What on earth was he hiding from me and why?

"Who's the client?"

"Oh no one you know," Carter replied, shoving his hand into his pocket. "They're new to town."

"He or she?" I demanded to know, my teeth starting to grind.

"He's definitely a he," he replied with a nervous cough. "It's a guy. Yep, a guy."

Narrowing my eyes on him, my pulse increased, and my nose tickled as tears threatened. He was most definitely hiding something, and I was scared to death that it was another woman—another woman whose arms I'd driven him in to.

"Should they really have a puppy if they don't have the money to buy it things?"

Carter shifted his feet and glanced up the aisle. "Well, you know how it is. Anyway, I'm going to go and let you carry on with your shopping." He leaned forward and kissed my cheek. "Let me know if there's anything you need, okay?"

His breath whispered against my skin and I instantly felt my body go on high alert at his closeness. All the familiar feelings were there—the butterflies in my belly, the tightening of my nipples and the pulsing between my legs. God, I wanted him. I felt horny as hell for him, but it seemed I'd most definitely peed on my own grits.

"Okay," I murmured as he pushed his cart away, leaving me thinking how sexy his ass was in his jeans.

When he disappeared my hands instinctively went to my belly and I felt bereft; alone and sad. My Carter didn't want me any longer.

After filling my cart with canned peaches and various flavors of licorice I decided I wasn't in the mood for any more shopping and made my way to the checkout. There was only one cashier working, Molly Callendar, who was married to Rueben, one of the six full time members of Dayton Valley's fire crew. There were two people in front of me, one being Talia Pitt, an old school friend of Ellie's who'd just returned to town after working and living in Boston for a couple of years. She had never been a friend of mine, we just always clashed for some reason, probably because I was Ellie's best friend and Talia had been desperate for the role.

She was beauty queen pretty, with long red hair and, due to their coloring, there were many people over the years who'd thought she and Carter would have been a good match—Talia included. With her curvy figure, enhanced boobs and perfectly made-up face, I would have agreed had I not been madly in love with the stupid, ginger, veterinary.

"Oh, hi," Talia said, her eyes instantly going to my belly which was definitely showing the baby growing inside it. "I hear congratulations are in order."

Her tone certainly didn't sound congratulatory. It sounded a little bitchy and when she flashed me a smile that just about twitched at her lips, I knew I was right.

"Thanks," I replied, forcing a return smile that actually showed my teeth. "It was a shock but we're really happy about it."

Talia's lip curled and she then scanned me up and down. "I'm sure. Although, you're not together I hear."

My heart flipped over and immediately I wanted to grab a hold of her and tell her to stay away from him. I knew Talia and was well aware going after Carter would definitely be on her agenda.

"We're just taking some time to get used to everything, but all's good." It was my turn to give a barely there smile. "I'm going over there after I've finished here, as a matter of fact."

"Good that you're still *friends*," Talia replied, emphasizing friends like it was a dirty word.

About to open my mouth, I stopped when the conveyor belt began to move, and Talia's items moved closer to Molly and the checkout.

"Well," Talia said, turning away from me. "Great catching up."

With her back to me my fingers twitched at the sight of her lustrous hair falling down her back. It was the most gorgeous auburn color, a little lighter than Carter's, and it was so full and bouncy I wanted to grab a hold of it and pull her back onto her ass.

Instead, I decided my time would be much better spent, loading my goods onto the conveyor belt. However, when I reached into the cart, Molly's voice stopped me.

"Hey, Bronte sweetie, don't bother getting them out."

I looked up and frowned at her. "Sorry."

"Don't get them out. Carter has arranged to pay for them and asked Dewey if we could deliver them to your house for you." She gave me the brightest smile and laid a hand against her heart. "He's so cute how he doesn't want you lifting anything."

"W-what?" I asked, glancing down at the twenty or so cans of peaches.

"He's gonna pay for them sweetie, and Dewey's gonna get Robbie to deliver them later."

She nodded over to the little office which was on a platform and looked over the three checkout desks. When I looked over, Dewey, the manager, gave me a wave.

"Just push your cart over to the office and we'll ring it up later. That okay, sweetie?" Molly beamed while my heart felt fuller than it had in a long while.

"He did that for me?" I whispered.

Talia, still in front of me, sighed. "Any chance we can move this along."

When I looked at her, there were most definitely hints of the green-eyed monster looking back at me. 'Well, tough titties,' I thought. Carter did *that* for *me*. Me and his baby. I'd be damned if I'd let anyone else muscle in on him, least of all Talia Pitt.

Looking back to Dewey, I saw he was beckoning me over with a huge grin on his face. I maneuvered my cart around Talia, accidently clipping her butt as I did.

"Thanks, Molly. See you again soon."

"Bye sweetie, you take care now."

As I waved bye to Molly, I didn't miss the fact that Talia was looking less than happy, and it made a girl's heart sing.

***

Taking a huge breath, I knocked on Carter's door, feeling apprehensive about visiting with him. It'd been a real nice gesture with my groceries, but I hadn't forgotten how strange he'd acted over the puppy things in his cart. He was definitely hiding something from me.

"Just a minute," Carter called from behind the closed door.

Biting my top lip, I waited anxiously for the door to be swung open.

"Lollipop," he exclaimed. "You're here." He glanced over his shoulder and moved into the hallway, pulling the door to almost closed behind him. "This is a surprise."

"I, erm, well I just wanted to say thank you for the groceries. It was a real kind thing to do."

Carter's face softened and a hand came up to take a hold of a lock of my hair. "Anything for you, Lollipop," he whispered. He smiled and raked his eyes over my face and hair. "God, I love your hair this color, but you know I kinda miss the blonde."

"Yeah? This has to stay for now. I can't dye it, so it'll have to grow out."

"You know, that's only the first trimester," Carter offered. "I read in my book that there's no real danger after that. You're three weeks into your second trimester, so you'd be safe."

"I don't know," I shrugged. "I'd rather be safe than sorry."

Carter opened his mouth to say something but was cut off by a high-pitched bark coming from behind the door.

"What was that?" I asked, trying to look over his shoulder through the gap in the doorway.

Carter's face blanched. "No-nothing," he stammered.

Yap, yap.

There it was again. "Carter, do you have a dog in there?" I pressed on his shoulder with the palm of my hand. He pushed back, but I was determined. "Seriously, let me in."

I pushed again and this time Carter sighed heavily and moved to one side. "It was supposed to be a surprise, once I'd got him house trained."

Rushing inside, I gasped with delight when the cutest little black and gold fluffy bundle came running to me. Her ears were long, but she had a short nose and cute button eyes.

"Oh, my God," I gasped. "She's gorgeous. What is she?"

"She is he," Carter replied, getting down onto the floor with me. "Definitely a Golden Retriever and not real sure of the other; possibly a Coonhound."

Picking up the little bundle, I could see where he was coming from.

"He's beautiful, babe. What's his name?" I looked over to Carter, my eyes shining—damn hormones.

Carter's head dropped and a little blush came to his face. "You can change it, if you want," he replied.

"Tell me," I urged.

He took a deep breath and his eyes met mine again. "Mani."

It was only a name, but my heart felt full to bursting with love for the gorgeous redhead in front of me. "You named him Mani? Oh my God, Carter, thank you so much." I flung myself at him, peppering kisses over his face. "He's gorgeous and he has the best name ever. I love the real Mani and I love this Mani too." I paused from kissing him, a thought hitting me in the head like a sledgehammer. "He is for me, isn't he?"

Carter's face softened. "Oh course, he's for you, Lollipop. I just wanted to have him all ready and trained before I gave him to you." He looked down at Mani and rubbed behind his ears. "It was to show you I could be responsible. If I could take care of a puppy, I could take care of a baby."

I began to laugh and stroked a hand down his cheek. "Thank you, it's a beautiful idea and I love him." I took in a deep breath. "And I love you too."

My lips parted, waiting for Carter to pounce but he just sat there looking at me. Love shone from his eyes, but the lust I was used to wasn't there. They were so void of it I was pretty sure I could've danced around naked with my hoo-hah lit up by fairy lights and he still wouldn't have made a move.

"Anyway," I sighed, feeling a little awkward. "I just wanted to say thank you for the groceries, and Mani of course."

"My absolute pleasure, Lollipop. You'll visit him, right. Until he's ready to come home with you, because I don't want you to have to do anything. No stress or worry, okay."

There was no hint that we might both be Mani's human parents together, here in Carter's apartment, and that hurt me. Problem was it was my own fault. I'd been the one to push him away and now I'd seen the light, it appeared that he'd got bored of waiting.

"Hey," Carter said. "I have an idea. Why don't you stay and visit with Mani? We can order takeout from the café and watch a movie. What do you say?"

Looking from him to Mani, I nodded. "That would be great. I'd like that."

"Excellent."

A couple of hours later after eating Delphine's lasagna, we curled up on the sofa and watched the Secret Life of Pets for about the fourth time. We both laughed at the antics of Max and his pals but all the time my heart felt heavy that Carter didn't want me any longer and the realization that I'd been a complete idiot.

CHAPTER 18

Carter

"**H**appy birthday, my baby." Mom squeezed my cheeks together and kissed me. "I can't believe you're twenty-seven. I still remember pushing you out and hearing that cute little scream of yours. Although, you do know you ruined me down there. Your dad said it looked like—"

"Mom, please," I groaned, interrupting her. "I don't want to have to think about your… well, just please don't."

Dad started to laugh, dropping his head back. "You remember honey, how he came out covered in shit." He turned to me. "Typical of you, you couldn't damn well wait. Just like now, when you gotta shit, you gotta shit."

"How did I not know that?" Ellie cried, clinking her beer bottle with Hunter's. "That's such good shit to have on him."

"Hah, quite literally." Hunter joined in with my dad's laughter. "Oh, you are so going to wish I didn't know that."

Throwing a glare at my best friend, I touched my ring finger and raised my brows. "Hey, Ellie," I called. I knew it was a dirty trick, but that fucker was not using my birth against me.

"Yeah."

Hunter narrowed his eyes on me and turned to my sister. "We probably shouldn't mention the poop thing again. He couldn't help it."

"What?" Ellie cried. "Are you turning soft on me, Delaney?"

"No, no." He frowned and shook his head. "I just think there's much better things we can burn him with."

He shot a gaze at me, a look that said this wasn't over. I knew that as soon as his proposal to Ellie was out of the bag all bets were off. Me shitting myself on the way out of my mom's cooch was not something that would go away.

Ellie shrugged and took a swig of her beer. "I guess so. The fact that he's ginger is enough."

"Hey," I cried. "There's nothing wrong with being ginger."

"Hmm," Ellie mused. "I kinda disagree. I mean the color is nice and everything, but everyone knows when it's you who was the last one to use the soap."

Hunter and Dad bust out laughing while Mom looked a little perplexed.

"How's that, sweetheart?" she asked.

"Really, Mom?" Ellie rolled her eyes. "You seriously don't get it?"

She shook her head as Dad put an arm around her shoulders. "It's to do with the color of his pubes, honey."

Mom looked at him for a beat and then gasped. "Ellie, that's disgusting. And don't give your brother crap about being ginger. His hair is beautiful. Anyway, I'd call it more titian than ginger."

"I don't care that I'm ginger," I cried. "Who wants to be a guy with boring brown hair." I looked pointedly at the handsome bastard standing next to me with his arm around my sister.

"Quite right," Dad agreed with a wink. "Besides you have so much more to look forward to than the guy with boring brown hair."

"Like what?" Ellie asked, brushing a hand over Hunt's hair and smiling at him with a soppy loved up look on her face.

"White hair," Dad cried followed with a roar of laughter that everyone except me joined in with.

"Very funny," I growled but with a sly grin on my face. You had to love my family.

Still chuckling to himself, Dad started to put the steaks on the grill when the side gate into the yard opened. The first sight I saw was the best birthday gift I could ever want; Bronte. She was dressed in denim shorts and a pink flowy top with cute little sleeves that did nothing to hide the bump she had her hand resting on, while the other held a gift bag. Behind followed her mom, dad and brother Austen.

"Hey everyone," her sexy voice called, but her eyes were on me.

As soon as she took a step onto the patio, Mani looked up from his chew toy and ran toward Bronte, yapping his delight at seeing her.

"Oh baby," she crooned, handing the bag off to me and dropping to her knees to give him a belly rub. Mani obliged by rolling over onto his back and kicking his legs with joy. "You miss me?"

My heart thudded an extra beat. He wasn't the only one, I'd barely seen her in the week since the day I'd paid for her groceries and we'd spent the evening watching a movie.

"Carter, he's grown so much."

I looked down at her and nodded. "I know and he's really missed you, Lollipop. You should come to the apartment to visit with him a little more."

She grinned and carried on scratching away at Mani's sweet spot. "Yes, I will. I've just been so busy this week with the salon."

When she looked up at me, she literally took my breath away. I exhaled what little air I still had left in my lungs and felt a crackle of electricity between us, as her big blue eyes blinked slowly. Her chest rose slowly up and down and her hand on Mani's belly trembled. We still had that connection, that sexual chemistry, but I had to prove to her that I could be the man she needed and the father our baby deserved.

"We'll eat as soon as Jefferson and the aunts get here," I said around clearing my throat.

"Oh. Yeah, no problem." Her eyes darted back down to Mani and the connection was broken.

It was at that moment that the silence between us was broken by the rest of the Delaney clan arriving.

***

A couple of hours later, all the food gone, everyone seemed to be pretty relaxed and having a good time. As far as birthdays went my twenty-seventh was turning out to be pretty good. I was spending it with everyone I cared about and I just hoped the following year, with my kid there, would be even better.

I'd had some pretty great gifts too, but the best had been a really cool digital stethoscope from Bronte. She knew mine had just been a cheap one I'd got when I first entered vet school, and I'd been promising myself a new one for ages. The fact that she'd remembered, had to mean something, didn't it?

Looking over to her, I was happy that she seemed okay. She was sitting with the rest of the women sipping on a glass of Mom's homemade lemonade and there was a big smile on her face. I'd done everything I could all day to make sure she didn't have to move or lift a finger. The fact that she looked relaxed meant I'd done my job.

"Hey, son," Dad called from the fire pit where he was talking with the guys. "Can you check if there's any more beers in the refrigerator inside and bring them to the outside one."

I nodded and walked toward the house. As I rounded the corner, I heard giggling and whispering and pulled up short, wondering who the hell it could be. I'd have put money on it being Ellie and Hunt, but I'd just seen them both in the yard with everyone else. Creeping quietly, I poked my head around the corner of the house and there outside our back door was Austen, making out with a girl. Not-so-little-any-longer, fourteen-year-old Austen who was well on his way to second base as his hand hovered over the girl's chest.

"What the hell is going on?" I cried.

Two heads parted, Austen's dirty blond one swung around to me while his hand still hung in the air over the boob of the black-haired girl who was desperately trying to bury her face in his chest.

"Carter," Austen gasped, his deep voice proving his balls had finally dropped. "It's not what you think."

"What that you were just about to get to second base. I bet not." I took a step closer to them and realized it was Doc Browning's youngest daughter, Peggy, who he'd been sucking the face off. "And you, Peggy, do your folks know you're here?"

The Doc and his family only lived a couple of blocks away, but it was almost dark, so I doubted whether she'd asked for permission to visit.

Peggy's head shot up. "They think I'm still over at Vicki's house two doors down. Please don't tell them."

Austen looked down at her and his face softened. "Carter won't spill, he's a good guy."

I kinda preened a little that Austen would say that about me, but even I knew he was probably playing me.

"Austin, I think you better make sure Peggy gets home, don't you?"

"It's okay," Peggy cried, grabbing hold of Austen's hand. "My dad is on his way to pick me up."

"You won't tell, will you, Carter?" Austen asked, his eyes begging me. "She's only been here a few minutes."

"He's telling the truth," Peggy added. "I was visiting with Vicki when Austen texted me that he was here."

Damn, they looked so scared and I was a sucker for young love.

"I won't say anything, but you best go wait for your dad." I nodded toward the gate leading out to the driveway. "Austen make sure Peggy gets into her dad's car—maybe, without him seeing you."

He nodded and grabbing her hand dragged her away from the house.

I was still smiling to myself when a few minutes later, Austen sidled up beside me.

"Can I ask you something?" He winced and scratched his head.

"Sure, but did Peggy's dad come get her?"

"Yeah, I waited but he didn't see me. So, can I ask you?"

With my beer paused at my mouth, I nodded, happy that he'd seen his girlfriend safe.

"How do you know if you're ready for sex."

The beer that had only just entered my mouth came shooting straight back out.

"You don't at fourteen, dude." I coughed, swiping at the beer dripping down my chin onto my tee.

"Yeah, but I'm kinda getting the feelings," Austen hissed putting his mouth closer to my ear. "You know, down there."

I blinked twice and then blew out a breath. "I... ah... I'm not sure... I guess."

"What's going on guys?" Hunter came between us and slapped a hand on each of our backs.

Looking at Austen, I pointed at him and blew out a breath before scrubbing my hand down my face.

"I'm asking Carter for advice," Austen whispered. "About s-e-x."

Hunter took a step back and looked at me. "You gave him advice about s-e-x."

"You do know it's my twenty-seventh birthday today," I cried. "You don't have to spell it out for me and why the fuck are we spelling it out anyway?"

"Hey, douchebag," Hunter growled and poked me in the ribs. "Kid on board."

"I'm fifteen," Austen replied. "I know cuss words."

"You're fourteen," Hunter and I chimed in unison. "And no," I added turning to Hunter. "I did not talk to him about sex. He asked, but I didn't say anything."

Austen kicked at the ground and pouted. "He was pretty lame actually."

Hunter chuckled and put an arm around Austen. "You really should have come to me, dude. Carter isn't the guy to talk about," he lowered his voice, glancing around the yard, "s-e-x with. I'm much more of an expert."

Austen raised a brow. "Well, he got my sister pregnant and he's a vet, so it figures that he'd know. I mean no disrespect, Hunter, but you still live with your pop."

I couldn't help the loud burst of laughter that busted right from the bottom of my gut. The great Hunter Delaney had been burned by a fourteen-year-old kid.

"You know what," Austen sighed. "I'm just gonna YouTube it, or maybe call Shaw at Harvard." He started to leave and then looked over his shoulder. "I should've known better than to ask either of you two. You both suck balls."

As Austen joined everyone else, I looked to Hunter.

"What the fuck?" He pointed to Austen. "He thinks YouTube is more informative about sex than us, the two hottest, most successful with women guys in Dayton Valley."

He was walking away, shaking his head in disbelief, when Bronte appeared next to me clutching an empty glass.

"Hey, Lollipop, you want more lemonade."

She gave me a small smile. "Yes, but I can get it."

"No, it's fine. You go and sit, and I'll do it."

As she passed me her glass my phone started to ring. "Hang on one sec." I looked down at the screen to see it was Nancy Andrews. It had been the apartment block maintenance meeting with the building's owner and superintendent that afternoon. I'd asked Nancy to raise the idea of putting a gate on the shared garden and adding a shaded area. I wanted to be able to take Mani out there and not have to worry about him running off. As for the shaded area, that was for when the baby came so they didn't get too much sun.

"Can I call you back?" I said as I answered the phone and looked up at Lollipop. I was anxious that I would be the one to get her lemonade for her. I wanted to do everything for her. "Or you could come around later?"

Nancy said it was no problem and she would push a copy of the meeting's minutes under my door and she then rang off.

As I put my phone back into my pocket, I opened my mouth to speak to Bronte, but she was already walking into the house.

"Hey, Lollipop, I said I'd get it."

She stopped and looked over her shoulder, her smile had gone, sadness in her eyes took me by surprise. "It's fine." She shrugged. "You're busy and I have to get used to doing things for myself."

Before I had time to respond, she turned and walked away and I suddenly felt as though we'd taken ten steps back, all over one glass of lemonade.

CHAPTER 19

Carter

Things with Bronte most definitely had taken a step backward, since my birthday. We'd conversed only by text and she'd had her mom pick Mani up and bring him to her house for the day instead of visiting my apartment.

Well, enough was enough. She couldn't avoid me any longer. I pulled up to her house, with Mani and the list of things I'd bought for the baby. I hadn't waited to check she was good with it; I'd just gone ahead bought the stuff and fuck the consequences. I was past giving her time; I was ready to take back what was mine.

"Carter," Bronte gasped as she opened the door. "What're you doing here?"

I raised a brow. "You're having my baby and contrary to what you think, I care. Plus, Mani wanted to see you."

I held up the cute black and gold fluff ball with my hand under his butt.

"Hey, sweet baby," she crooned and tickled him under his chin.

I felt slightly uncomfortable in the pants department as an image of her doing the same thing to my balls, flashed through my head. Ball and dick work were my girl's specialty for sure. I often wondered how she'd gained her skills, I mean it wasn't the kind of thing they taught at Girl Guides, was it?

The door opening wider brought me back to reality.

"You best come in."

Stepping into the wide hallway, I put Mani down on the floor and watched as he skidded on the tiles, desperate to get to Bronte. The little guy had taste; I'd give him that. She bent to pick him up and gave me a quick flash of cleavage, surprising me at how full and big her boobs were.

"Shit, Lollipop," I groaned. "You want me to bust my pants."

Straightening up with Mani in her arms, she narrowed her eyes at me. "You shouldn't be looking."

"Yeah, and like that will happen. That's like asking a kid not to eat just ice cream at an all you can eat buffet."

"My titties are not part of a buffet, thank you very much."

I tilted my head to one side and laid my eyes firmly on them. "At my imaginary buffet they are. In fact," I said with a sigh, "I think they'd probably be my death row meal."

She rolled her eyes, but I didn't miss the slight smile that stretched her pretty pink lips. A tiny movement but even so, it gave me hope that maybe I was back in the race.

"Apart from bringing Mani to see me, and caring about the baby," Bronte said as she moved down the hallway. "What is it that brought you around? Because I know you, Carter Maples. There's something else."

Putting Mani on the floor next to a basket of dog toys, she looked over her shoulder at me and grinned. "I couldn't resist getting them for when he visited."

Her words made my chest clinch. I didn't want him visiting. I wanted him living with me; me, Lollipop and the baby. I got that she was being cautious, but I didn't understand how she still didn't trust my word that she and the baby were what I wanted.

"He certainly looks happy." I nodded to where Mani was playing, pushing away the words I really wanted to say.

We both watched our boy for a few seconds, loving smiles on both our faces, until Bronte took a seat on the sofa and I plonked down next to her.

"Okay, spill it."

I reached inside my jacket pocket and pulled out my list. "I got these things and wanted you to know, so that way you didn't buy them too."

I passed the paper to her and watched as she read through everything.

"Carter, this must have cost you a fortune. You didn't need to get all of this." Her mouth dropped open into a perfect o as she looked up at me. "That's so generous but I figured we could just get a travel crib for your apartment. It'd be much simpler than you having to set up a nursery."

I breathed out slowly, trying hard to hold onto my temper. It was about time she realized this wasn't a part-time gig for me. We were having a baby together—a phrase with no truer meaning.

"We are having a baby," I replied, my tone low. "The key word being 'we'. That means us, together, which also means we are not doing this separately. I don't care whether it takes you until the moment that you're pushing him or her out, but you will realize that we are a family. One way or another, Lollipop, when you leave the hospital with that baby it will be to come home to our apartment. An apartment that will have a cute little nursery for our child. You get me?"

Inhaling slowly, she watched me carefully, her eyes staring into mine, reading the truth in them. I held my breath, the words of reasoning already formed in my head for when she denied me. Surprising me though, her blue and purple waves bobbed as she nodded once and then twice.

"Prove yourself to me and it's a deal," she whispered, her pointy little chin wobbling slightly.

I wanted to throw my arms in the air and scream that I'd surely done enough to damn well prove how much I wanted her and the baby. However, I'd learned enough over the past few weeks to know that wasn't the way to deal with a hormonal Bronte.

"I will." Smiling, I expected her to at least give me one back. Instead, she burst into tears with a loud howl that shocked Mani into dropping his rubber chicken.

"Hey," I soothed, pulling her against me. "What's wrong?"

"I don't know," she sobbed against my shoulder. "I just want to cry."

"That's okay, honey. You just cry."

"But you don't know what it's like." She pushed me away from her and I caught sight of one of the weirdest, crying faces that I'd ever seen. God, I loved that woman more than anything, but shit she was an ugly crier.

"I have fat ankles, my back hurts, all I want to eat are canned peaches and licorice and I've never felt so horny in all my damn life." Another howl left her mouth and as it did, I was a little bothered to see a snot bubble.

Reaching inside my pocket I pulled out a napkin. Admittedly it was a little dirty as I'd used it to wipe tuna mayo from around my mouth, but if I folded that part over, she'd be good to go.

Not seeing, or caring, Bronte snatched it from my hand and proceeded to blow her nose on it.

"You got me into this mess," she whimpered and gave another blow and a wipe. "And why can I smell fish?"

"No idea. Put your legs up on me," I said, quickly changing the subject. "Let me rub your feet for you."

Narrow eyes stared back at me, pure venom glinting out through the tiny slits of blue.

"I didn't say my feet hurt," she snapped. "Were you even listening to me?"

"I just thought it would help," I offered.

"Oh yeah," she scoffed, squeezing the even dirtier tissue into a ball and throwing it back at me. "Like you thought it was a good thing to stick that mammoth penis of yours into my vagina and leave a little gift behind."

"You didn't exactly pooh, pooh, the idea, Lollipop."

Wrong thing to say because a cushion came flying toward me.

"Shit, that hurt."

"As if," she snarled. "It's a damn cushion, Carter. How can a cushion hurt?"

"Well, if it's thrown at point blank range straight at my face it can." Rubbing at my forehead I groaned. "You know, Lollipop, you really have to stop throwing things at me. With the number of objects that you keep launching at me, I'll have brain issues before the baby even gets here."

"Well stop being an idiot and I might."

She pouted like a little girl who'd had her toys taken away and I felt a little sorry for her. Everything was changing with her body and it must have been real weird; still didn't justify her using me as target practice though.

"Okay," I said with a sigh. "Let's talk about the positive aspects of being pregnant." I thought about what she'd said and the sudden realization that she was desperate for me, left me more than a little excited. My dick was most definitely waking up to that fact. "I mean you said you feel horny right? We can certainly do something about that."

I pulled her into my arms, and just as my lips landed on hers, the door opened, followed by a loud groan.

"Really," Austen cried. "That's what got you into trouble in the first place."

Bronte pulled away and shoved me in the chest. "We were wrestling is all."

Austen shook his head. "I told you before, I know what sex is. Ask Carter."

Her gaze shot to mine and wide eyes stared at me. "What does he mean? Ask Carter if he knows about sex."

I threw Austen a look that thanked him for, one, busting in on us and, two, throwing me under the damn school bus he went on every day because yes, he was only fourteen and didn't need to be thinking about s-e-x.

"He doesn't mean anything. Do you, Austen?"

Catching my drift, he shook his head. "I guess not. I guess I'm just the kid brother who knows nothing about anything. The one who doesn't know where babies come from. The one who has no damn idea what a hard on is."

Dropping my head into my hands, I groaned. The kid had just thrown himself under the bus with me. We were about to be squashed together.

"Austen. How the hell do you know that... I told Mom not to worry about you, do I have to get Dad to give you the talk?"

"God no," he yelled. "Please no. He's probably better than Carter or Hunter, but I'd rather die a virgin than talk to Dad about it. You know what,

I'm just gonna go back to my room and pretend this never happened and that I'm not hungry or want to know when Mom will be back to make dinner."

He threw us a wave and was gone, leaving a distinct atmosphere in the room. One that said if I didn't get out of there quick or change the subject, I was going to be blamed for teaching him about sex. Not that that particular conversation had gone too well.

"So," I said cheerfully. "How about the Easter Fayre, you think you might run for Easter Queen this year, Lollipop?"

"Oh my God, I hate you," she bawled. "Who wants an Easter Queen with cankles and gas?"

CHAPTER 20

Bronte

"Hey, Jefferson," I sighed as he opened the door to his house at The Big D ranch. "How're you doing?"

He smiled brightly and smoothed a hand over his hair, sweeping it back from his face. He was most definitely hot for an older guy, but despite what I'd led Ellie to believe a few months back, he was not my type. The hair was the wrong color for one; definitely not red enough.

"I'm good thanks, honey. I'm just off to the new piece of land to put some fencing up with Tom and Sam." He placed his cowboy hat on his head and gave me a fatherly wink. "You here to see Ellie, 'cause she's over in the barn with Hunter. They're picking floor covering," he said with a smirk and a little shake of his head. "Well, arguing about wooden flooring versus tiles."

"All getting a little tense, right?"

I knew Ellie and was pretty sure that she'd have a spreadsheet and a scrapbook full of things for the new house and was stressing over every little detail.

"Ah it's all good," he replied. "I'm just happy I don't have to be any part of it, but I'll be glad when Hunt gets his mind back on the job. He's a little distracted."

"Hmm." I shrugged. "Moving in together is a big commitment. As long as he's not having second thoughts because then I may just have to cut off his balls."

Jefferson laughed and moved down the porch steps. "No chance of that. My boy is totally gone for that girl. Anyways, I'd best get going. Go on in if you want. Janice and Lynn are cooking soup in the kitchen—I think it's pork and blueberry today." He grimaced. "Oh, and if you do, don't take your shoes off that damn dog of theirs will chew it to its death."

"Oh my gosh," I squealed. "They have a puppy. You know Carter got me a puppy, right?"

"Where'd you think he got him." Jefferson raised a brow. "Okay so, I'll see you later honey."

With that he was gone, jogging down the porch steps and over to his truck which was loaded with fencing materials and now had Sam and Tom leaning against it.

As his vehicle pulled away, I gave a courtesy knock on the door and walked in.

"Aunt J, Aunt L, you back there?"

A silver head poked around the door. I knew it was Hunter's Aunt Lynn-Ann because I'd figured a while ago that she wore her parting to the right.

"Why Bronte, sweetheart, so lovely to see you. You want to come through and taste our new soup?"

The thought of pork and blueberry didn't settle right on my stomach, so I laid a hand against it and shook my head.

"A little nauseous today, Aunt L."

"Oh no, morning sickness, sweetheart?"

"Hmm," I lied, seeing as I'd barely had any at all. Something I counted myself lucky for. "I managed to keep some toast down."

"Well come on through anyway, we're just finishing up."

As I wandered through to the living room, I heard snuffling and growling, and sure enough in the middle of the rug was a cute little puppy. It looked exactly like Mani and was, as Jefferson warned me, chewing on a shoe.

"Oh, he's adorable." Dropping to my knees I rolled the pup over and scratched his belly, just like my own little guy loved. "What's his name."

"Primrose," Aunt L replied.

When I looked up at her she was grinning from ear to ear.

"He's gorgeous, isn't he?" She clutched at her pale blue blouse and stared down at the puppy. "I think even Jefferson is getting attached."

Taking another quick look between Primrose's legs I confirmed it was most definitely a 'he'.

"Primrose?" I asked.

"Yes, we thought he was a girl. You know that sneaky Carter tried to swap him out for the female puppy, but we spotted it, didn't we, Janice-Ann?"

Aunt J appeared next to her sister, wiping her hands on a towel. "We did. The female was all black for a start."

Both sisters moved into the room and sat themselves down on the sofa.

"So, how are you, Bronte, dear?" Aunt J asked, the conversation about their male dog being called Primrose swiftly forgotten.

"I'm good thank you." As Primrose went back to chewing, I got onto my feet and moved to an armchair. "Getting used to the idea, you know."

The two sisters gave me sympathetic smiles and sighed.

"Please, don't be sorry for me. I truly am getting used to the idea. And I'm looking forward to it all, except the birth of course."

"Oh, we're not sorry you're having a baby, honey," Aunt J replied. "Just thinking you must be worried, with Carter being the daddy and all."

"Worried?" Apprehension gnawed at my gut, wondering why they'd say such a thing. "What's wrong with Carter? What have you heard?"

"Nothing," Aunt J replied, reaching out and patting my hand. "He's a perfectly lovely boy—well most of the time."

Aunt L touched her hair. "We mean the ginger, dear."

"God, no," I cried relaxing back into the chair, relieved that was all it was. "I love his hair."

"Well, God willing your baby will be blonde, like you." Aunt J frowned and looked at my head. "When you're not dying it's all kinds of silly colors."

"Something is worrying you though. We can see it can't we Janice-Ann?"

Aunt J nodded. "Most definitely. So, what is it that's troubling you?"

I'd gone to see Ellie and talk things through with her, but she was busy. Therefore, I decided there'd be no harm in telling two ladies in their sixties all about my romance troubles.

"I think Carter has gone off me and might be falling for Nancy Andrews," I blurted out, relieved at getting it off my chest.

The two aunts both tinkled a laugh and scoffed at me.

"Carter and Nancy." Aunt L waved a dismissive hand at me. "Ridiculous. She's far too young for him."

"She's the same age as Shaw," I offered. "That's not so young."

Aunt L shook her head. "Nope. No way. I'm not having it. Carter is a little shit most of the time, except to you. You're the only one I've ever seen him be nice to."

"To be fair," Aunt J offered. "He's always sweet as pie to us."

"Very true. Oh, and his mom and dad." Aunt L tilted her head and paused, thinking. "You know, it's actually mainly Ellie he's a little shit with."

The three of us nodded in agreement.

"You don't think I need worry about Nancy?" I asked, wondering why on earth I thought they'd know.

"I doubt it, dear," Aunt L replied. "Nancy went on a date with Minnesota on Saturday, anyway."

"She did," I gasped. "How do you know that, and I don't?"

Aunt L smiled. "You need to go to bingo night, dear. You get all the gossip there."

Baffled at how a bunch of old people knew the town's dating gossip, I nodded and determined to get out a bit more.

"I guess he just doesn't want me then," I groaned, dropping my head to my hands.

"Of course, he does," Aunt J sighed. "But maybe you need to show him you want him. You were the one who ended things, were you not?"

"Well, yes, but I feel stupid now. I'm worried it's too late."

"It's never too late," Aunt L replied as she stood. "Give him what all men want; sex."

I gasped, shocked at her response. As far as I knew neither of the aunts had ever been married, but I supposed that didn't make them virgins.

"Lynn-Ann is right, Bronte. You need to go around there with some nice panties and bra on and seduce him."

"I agree with Janice-Ann and I thoroughly recommend black, or maybe a nice deep purple color."

As I stared, open-mouthed at both the aunts, the door clattered open and Ellie and Hunter rushed in. They were both breathless, Hunter's hair was a mess, and Ellie's t-shirt was most definitely inside out.

"You finally manage to decide on a flooring you like?" Aunt L asked.

"Oh, hey, Bronte." Ellie gave me a wave. "Ah, yep. Hunt decided I was right in the end."

"You see," Aunt L said pointing at them. "Sex gets you everything you want. Now, who'd like some tea?"

CHAPTER 21

Carter

*P*ig shit stinks—fact!

Lance Dickinson was the worst man on the planet—
fact!

He knew how I hated going out to Jim Wickerson's pig farm, yet somehow, he always worked it that I was the only one available.

I was already pissed at him because while he'd finally made a decision about the partnership—almost a month after I'd met with him about it, he was taking his goddamn sweet time in getting the paperwork drawn up. Add to the fact he'd suddenly had a house call to make which meant I was sticking Jim's damn feeder piglets with a vaccination, while up to my ankles in shit. Pigs were dirty and shit and pissed wherever they cared to.

"Get you a cold one, Carter?" Jim asked.

"That'd be good, Jim, thanks." I turned back to the piglet wriggling around in my arms and pushed the skin forward on his neck, just below his ear. When I jabbed in the needle it squealed blue murder. "There you go." I set it back on his feet and looked in the pen to find that had been the last one.

"All done?" Jim came beside me and peered in. "You were real quick today."

"Yeah, I guess I was." I glanced at an old clock up on the barn wall and realized he was right. I'd only taken thirty-five minutes to vaccinate fifteen piglets, some of which had been real wrigglers. "Got to be a record, I reckon."

"Reckon so. Now, I'll get you that drink because I'd be grateful if you'd also take a look at that five-month-old that was tail biting."

"It any better?" I asked, putting everything back into my bag and disposing of the needles in the Sharpsafe.

"Some." Jim shrugged and made his way out of the pig enclosure. "He's stopped biting, but it doesn't appear to be healin' much."

"Okay, I'll take a look. He in the isolation pen still, in the other barn?"

Jim nodded and made his way to the house, leaving me to go back to my truck and get some things I thought I might need. When I was closing the back tailgate, I noticed a little pink car winding its way up the track towards the farm.

"Bronte?" I murmured to myself as I watched her hit a rut and then swerve to avoid Jim's big, fat, Tom cat, Weasel.

Even from where I was standing, a least a couple of hundred feet away, I could see she was cursing about the state of the road surface. Jim didn't have a big farm, with a herd of hogs and sows large enough to service the butcher shops of the towns in our county and a couple of restaurants in Middleton Ridge. That meant that the track leading up to the farm was the least of his worries and he spent little or no money on it. This also meant that Bronte's car could possibly need a repair job, especially if she kept driving down it at the speed she was.

Grimacing as she almost did a wheel spin when she stopped next to my truck, I rubbed a hand over my head as apprehension hit me. Why the hell had she come all the way out to Jim's to see me. I didn't think I'd done anything wrong since our last meeting, but her moods were so up and down, it was difficult to know.

"Lollipop?" I took a step forward as she slammed her car door.

"Does Jim know how dangerous that damn track is?" she asked, her arm going behind her to point in the direction she'd just come. "I hit my head on the roof of my car, twice."

I tried not to smirk. Her hair was piled high, so I doubted she'd felt a thing.

"You're okay though?" I asked.

"Yes," she snapped and looked down at the ground, her sneakers stark white against the brown stinking mess. "I wanted to see you."

"I guessed so," I replied wondering whether I should offer her my spare Wellington boots. "But why?"

Wide eyes stared back at me. "Well, why wouldn't I?"

"It's just you never come visit me at work usually. So, why today?"

I ran a hand through my hair and as I did, I heard the gasp and inhale. There was no disguising it, she was damn well turned on. All I'd done was straighten the mess on top of my own head. Feeling on top of my game I stretched my back muscles, knowing my Dayton Veterinary Clinic polo shirt would ride up enough to show a glimpse of skin. Skin and the happy trail that Bronte loved to follow. My eyes went to her rack, covered in a thin, white tank, under which I could clearly make out a plain bra with lace edging it. As I homed in on her titties, her nipples hardened pretty much instantly.

Oh yeah, she was turned on to the point of exploding.

Problem was I'd vowed that I'd prove what we had was so much more than lust.

"So?" I prompted, desperately trying not to think of her underneath me.

She looked around and then back toward Jim's house, before landing her gaze back on me—my dick to be more precise. Just having her eyes on it made it perk up a little, and as it pushed against my uniform cargo pants, she definitely noticed. She gave another little sigh followed by a peek of the tip of her tongue as it licked along her lips.

Images of what else that tongue could do filled my head and my dick went to full attention—well as much as it could without being free of the confines of my underwear and pants. Desperately, trying to steady my breathing I took a long inhale, and then slowly let the air go, hoping it might deflate my excitement.

No such damn luck. It grew painfully harder.

Bronte took a step forward and held out her hand as though she was going to give me a crotch hug. "Carter, I'm so damn horny," she gasped. "I really need you to have sex with me *now*."

As her delicate fingers flexed, I stepped to one side, grabbing my bag from the bed of the truck and shoving it in front of me to cover my excitement.

"No," I replied, my voice cracking. "Not happening, Lollipop."

"Please." Her face crumpled as though she might cry. "That's why I came. I have to have sex today, otherwise I might just... I don't know... combust."

I shook my head, even though my determination was ebbing with every second that her nipples pushed harder against her tank.

"I'm working."

"Never stopped you before," she groaned, stopping inches from me. "What about the time I gave you a blow job at the clinic? You were supposed to be working then but you couldn't wait to get your penis out."

"That was different," I protested, moving another step away from her. "I was working late, doing paperwork. I wasn't about to examine a pig that bites its own tail."

"Well, you sure look as though you want to have sex with me." Grabbing my hand that was holding the bag, she exposed my crotch which was indeed bulging. "*See!*"

My resolve was almost gone, especially when I looked her up and down. Her tits looked high and round and her legs long and smooth in denim shorts, already open at the button.

"Fuck," I groaned.

Bronte saw she had me on the ropes and smiled seductively. "I need you so bad, babe. You're the only one who knows how to satisfy me."

Shit she was good. I'd been so damned determined that I'd prove we were more than sex, but she'd enticed me like Eve had with Adam; getting him to eat that damn apple with her. Contemplating where we could go, I looked around but there was nowhere that didn't stink of or had some covering of pig shit.

"The truck," Lollipop said, reading my mind.

As she moved for my vehicle, something hit me. I wasn't actually willing to have sex with her, no matter how painful and blue my balls were. Whether it was catching sight of her little pot belly poking out from under her tank and knowing that was our baby was in there or the fact that in a pen, in my eyeline, a boar with the biggest balls I'd ever seen, had just mounted a sow, I had no idea, but whatever it was made me turn around and stop her.

"No, Lollipop. It isn't happening."

She pulled up short and gasped loudly, her face morphing into an expression of sheer horror.

"*What?*"

"I said it's not happening," I replied with a shrug. "We're not having sex in the back of my truck on a pig farm."

"I know that," she cried. "Did you think I wanted you to take me here." She flung her arm around. "It smells of pig poop. I thought we'd drive somewhere."

"Lollipop, I'm working. I can't drive off and leave Jim, just so I can have sex with you."

"But why not?"

"Because…" I struggled for the words, mainly because I was shocked that I was even turning her down in the first place. Old Carter would have given Jim some story about an emergency, driven up to the old make out point at Devil's Creek and made her scream with pleasure. "Because you're having a baby."

Yep, it was pretty lame even for me.

"I know, and whose fault is that?" Lollipop's eyes were murderous as she pointed a long, delicate finger at me. "Yours. You're the one who put this baby inside me. This baby that's making my hormones go crazy. It's your fault all I can think of is your damn penis. So, you need to do something about it, *Mister!*"

"We're not even together," I responded, giving her a one shoulder shrug.

Yeah, your damn choice, Lollipop.

"I thought that's what you wanted," she snapped, crossing her arms over her chest and obliterating my perfect view. "You said we could still have sex."

Narrowing my eyes at her I tried to recall our conversation. "That was weeks ago, and I only suggested it because I was shocked that you dumped me."

"I didn't dump you," she ground out. "I said we had to take it slow. That you had to be sure."

"And I told you I was, so…" I held my palms up and waited for a response, but she had nothing because she knew I was right. There was no damn reason on earth why we weren't together.

"Ugh," she eventually groaned. "You're so irritating at times. I don't know why I bother with you, I really don't. In fact, I'm not sure I even want to speak to you ever again. We should converse through our parents in future."

Geez, someone's hormones were rampant today. The woman was completely irrational. Her actually begging me for sex was crazy enough, but never speaking to me for the foreseeable future—like that was going to happen. Aside from us having a kid together, she was too damn addicted to my dick to never ask for it again.

"Lollipop," I sighed. "Why don't you go home, put your feet up and chill."

Wrong thing to say. Once again, the mouth moved before the brain even had a chance to consider whether I was spouting wise words, or not. Why didn't I learn? Why did I always put myself on the back foot with the gorgeous but fucking angry woman I loved?

Her nostrils flared, her eyes went wild like a bull about to rampage and as she lifted her leg to stamp her foot, I knew instantly it was a huge mistake.

"No, Lollipo—"

She couldn't have picked a bigger puddle of pig piss and shit if she'd gone around the farm and measured them individually. It was almost of tidal wave proportions, splashing up her legs, over her amazing tits and all over her face.

Who knew one petulant act could cause such devastation?

I tried not to find it funny, but as water dripped off the end of her nose and down her chin, I couldn't help letting out a loud belly laugh.

"Oh my God, Lollipop that's just so—"

"Don't say another word," she ground out, closing her eyes. "Not, one word."

Reaching into my pocket, I pulled out a handkerchief. "Here, let me help." I dabbed her face, but all I seemed to be doing was spreading the piss and shit across her face.

"Leave it. Just leave it," Bronte breathed out, her chin quivering. "I'm going home."

"So, the offer of sex is definitely off the cards then?" I asked, smirking.

Wild eyes flashed open as she gasped in shock that once again, I'd not engaged my brain. I was ready for the onslaught, but when a huge blob of shit dropped from the end of Bronte's nose onto her bottom lip, I figured it was time to make myself scarce.

CHAPTER 22

Bronte

Dayton Valley's Easter fayre was pretty much the biggest social event of the year. Mainly for the high school kids because when the fayre closed down at ten, they all congregated down at Fiddler's Field to drink, dance and generally have fun. In our senior year there was reckoned to be over two hundred kids down there. A ton of kids from Middleton Ridge Academy turned up, thinking their shit didn't stink and their guys started throwing their weight around. Obviously, those from Dayton Valley High weren't going to let that slide and a huge fight broke out—girls included. Ellie and I made a heap of cash that night placing bets with those not fighting on what time the Sheriff and his boys would turn up and a few side bets who'd get banged up the worse. Since then, things had calmed down a little, mainly because out of towners were no longer allowed access—the Sheriff always had a couple of guys keeping watch letting the kids do their own thing but being around if things got out of hand.

The point being it was a day everyone looked forward to throughout the year. The adults got drunk in the beer tent that Penny ran, while the kids played the games, went on the rides and made themselves sick with all the junk food for sale. We were a small town and pretty much shut down for the day so everyone could have fun.

However, looking at myself in the long mirror on my wall, my usual excitement for the day just wasn't there. My stomach looked like I'd eaten three portions of Mom's fried chicken *with* mac 'n' cheese. There was no way my jeans were going to fasten. Groaning I stomped over to my closet, wondering what I could wear.

Call me stupid but I wanted to look sexy. Ellie and I were meeting up with Hunter, Carter and a few of our friends and after the fiasco at Jim Wickerson's pig farm I needed to up my game.

I'd been mortified at begging him for sex, not least because it had resulted in me being covered in pee and poop. My feelings had also been hurt because he'd turned me down and I was determined he wouldn't again. Yeah, I was still incredibly horny and permanently turned on.

Who knew extra genital blood flow was a thing?

Flicking through the hangers on my rail, I heaved out a sigh of frustration.

"You're not ready."

It was Ellie and when I turned to look at her, I wanted to scream like a toddler who'd dropped its popsicle. She looked beautiful, just like I wanted to. Her hair was shiny and full, flowing down over her shoulders and almost touching her ass. While she was wearing the tiniest pair of denim shorts and a tight tee, tied in a knot at her waist that had the slogan, '*My Cowboy Rides Hard*'.

"Ugh," I groaned. "I see you're still getting plenty."

"Good morning to you too," she chimed back, throwing herself onto my bed. "How come you're so happy today?"

I pointed down at my bump which, while not huge, was not the flat stomach I was used to. "I can't fit into any of my clothes. These are my fat jeans and the button still won't fasten."

"Yeah well," Ellie muttered. "Your fat jeans are another woman's skinnies." She peered at my stomach and then nodded to my dresser. "Hair tie will do it. Loop it around the button through the hole then back around the button."

I did as she suggested and let out a momentary sigh of relief, before realizing I had no clue what to wear on top. My boobs had gotten huge and nothing would stretch across them bar a few tanks and tees. Reading my mind Ellie pointed to the door.

"Shaw must have a shirt that will fit you. A nice plaid one over the top of your tank. Leave the shirt open. When you've done that, I'll tie the laces on your sneakers for you."

"I'm not that fat I can't reach my feet," I cried, not really sure I could.

"Whatever." She reached for the magazine on my bed and started to flick through it. "Just hurry up, I need a breakfast burrito."

"You could have had breakfast at home, you know." I looked into the mirror to touch up my lip gloss and then fussed with my loose braid, positioning it over my shoulder.

"It's tradition. Benny's breakfast burrito, a weak cup of coffee and then straight on to the Ferris wheel. Hey, you going on that this year?"

"I still have five months to go, Ellie. I'm not likely to give birth up there if that's what you're worried about."

She tapped at the screen of her phone and sighed. "I'm not, I just didn't know if you were *allowed* to go on it, being pregnant. That's Hunter." She flashed me her phone screen. "He and Carter are at the field now, so hurry up."

Rolling my eyes, I padded back to my closet and pulled out a red and navy plaid shirt, giving it a sneaky little sniff before pulling it on and rolling up the sleeves.

"So, you already had something to wear?" Ellie said as I snatched up my keys from my dresser.

I shook my head. "Nope. You gave me the idea and I just happen to have this in my closet."

"Hmm," she replied, eying me as she got up from my bed. "Looks expensive. Shaw must be making good money bussing tables at that fancy restaurant he works weekends."

I didn't reply but led her from my room. She didn't need to know it was Carter's and that it made me feel like I was in his arms; she'd only give me shit about it.

***

As we walked through the gates into the field, my joy was complete when the first person we bumped into was Talia Pitt. She was wearing the skimpiest summer dress and the most ridiculously high wedge heels for walking around a dry and rutted field.

"Shit, is she allowed out during sunlight?" Ellie hissed from the corner of her mouth. "Hey, Talia, great to see you."

"I thought she was your friend?" I asked as Queen Bitch walked toward us, waving at Ellie.

"She was but Hunter told me they made out once when we were seventeen. It was a game of spin the bottle at Fiddler's field after the fayre. He said she was a grade one clinger. Talia, honey, how're you doing?"

"Ellie. Great to see you. I hear you finally snagged that cowboy every girl in town wants."

Flicking her hair over her shoulder, Ellie tinkled out a laugh. "I sure did. He's just." She sighed and clutched her shirt over her heart. "Wonderful."

Talia shivered and stretched her neck, obviously mortified at the thought of my friend boning Hunter. "Lovely," she ground out and then turned to me. "And my haven't you…" She looked down at my stomach and circled her finger in the air. "Blossomed. Quite the lump you have there."

"Yes," I replied through a gritted smile. "My *bump* is coming along nicely. Carter and I are so excited."

"Really," she exclaimed looking over her shoulder. "He didn't mention it when I was just visiting with him, over at Benny's stall."

Ellie and I looked at each other and then turned to stare across the field to where there was already a line at Benny's. Hunter and Carter were standing to one side talking to a group of four girls. I recognized one as Mindy Parkinson, an ex-hook up of Carter's and when he leaned in to say something close to her ear, I felt the already irrational hormones invading my body, turn a fiery red.

"We should get over there," Ellie replied, grabbing hold of my hand and tugging me. "The boys will be getting hungry."

Not bothering to say goodbye to Talia I chased after my best friend. We'd almost reached them when Austen came running up to us.

"Hey, sis. If you see Mom and Dad, you haven't seen me. Okay?"

I pulled Ellie to a stop. "Hang on. Why? What you up to?"

He glanced around the field and as I watched his eyes linger in a corner by the Slip 'n' Slide, I spotted Peggy Browning. Her gaze seemed to be most definitely in my little brother's direction.

"Is she why you don't want me to tell Mom and Dad I've seen you?"

Austen colored up and shifted his feet. "No."

"Oh my God," Ellie cried. "Peggy is why you were asking Carter and Hunter for sex advice, isn't she?"

"So, you did talk to Carter, about sex." I hissed at Austen, before swiveling around to look at Ellie. "He asked those two idiots for sex advice?" I then turned back to my brother. "Why didn't you ask me and Ellie? We could have given you some real good stuff to work on."

Austen took a step back and grimaced. "Ugh no. The point is you haven't seen me. Okay. Oh, and Ellie," he said curling his lip at her. "Tell Hunter he's a snitch and I won't be asking for his help again. He was pretty crappy anyways."

Ellie gasped. "Hunter is *the* best at sex. How can you say he was crappy? There is nothing crappy about Hunter where sex is concerned."

"Ellie, please," I groaned and then turned back to Austen. "Actually, what the hell are you doing asking about sex? You're fourteen."

"Fifteen." He grumbled and turned to walk away. "I'm not going to do anything stupid, don't worry."

"Make sure you don't," I called after him. "You're only fourt-."

"Fifteen, yeah, yeah, I know." He waved me away and then jogged off in the direction of Peggy who was looking at him like he was a long, cold drink in a desert. God, the kids started young nowadays.

"How could you not tell me that my little brother was asking for sex advice?"

Ellie shrugged and carried on her path toward her cowboy. "Didn't have a chance and it's not like either of those two will have given him any good tips."

"I thought you said that Hunter was great at sex. There's nothing crappy about Hunter where sex is involved is what you said."

"There isn't, but you really think he or my brother telling Austen to 'make sure you give it to her good and mix up the positions during every session, buddy', is what he needs to hear." She threw her hands in the air. "They'd never think to tell him to whack off before his first time to make it last longer, or to imagine her nipple is a juicy popsicle. Am I right?"

She had a point and her voice, a cross between Carter and Hunter, was pretty spot on to be fair. Not feeling the need to say anything else, we continued on. As we reached them, my heart tumbled as I saw Mindy smile and wink at Carter and then walk away with her group of friends.

"Hey, baby." Hunter immediately pulled Ellie into his arms and kissed her hard. It was so full on it even made me blush.

"Lollipop, you want the breakfast burrito?"

My tumbling heart actually deflated and fell right down to the pit of my stomach. He hadn't noticed I was wearing his shirt, or that I'd taken extra time on my hair and make-up. Actually, he wasn't even looking at me, but his gaze was over my shoulder.

"Hang on, hold that, I just need to catch up with…" He didn't finish his sentence, but when I turned to watch him, Carter had run over to chat to a group of women I recognized from my yoga group. I say my yoga group, Ellie and I had been twice but after Ellie farted in downward dog position, she never wanted to set foot in the place again. Like a good friend I supported her, and we'd decided to drink wine at Stars & Stripes between seven-thirty and eight-forty-five every Tuesday instead.

"So, you ladies want the usual?" Hunter asked, evidently having had his fill of Ellie for the time being.

"Hmm?" I asked, distractedly, my eyes still on Carter laughing with the yoga women.

"Breakfast burrito?" Hunter smiled and tugged at my elbow.

I turned to him and narrowed my eyes. "What's Carter doing with those women? And why was Mindy all giggly with him."

Hunter cleared his throat. "Not sure what you mean," he said, with a shake of his head before turning to Ellie. "Breakfast burrito, cutie pie?"

Hunter's face told me something was going on, and the fact that Carter couldn't wait to get away from me, told me everything I needed to know.

"You know what," I said, putting a hand on Hunter's arm. "I'm feeling a little queasy, so you both get breakfast and I'll catch you later."

"Bronte," Ellie whined. "It's tradition."

"Yeah, well I'm just not feeling like it." I leaned in and kissed her cheek. "Our parents are over there, so I'll catch you later."

"You sure?" She wrapped me in a hug. "Meet you at the Ferris wheel in say, twenty minutes?"

I nodded but was thinking I'd probably catch up with my folks and then sneak back home. Carter was obviously moving on, publicly. I for one didn't want to watch it. Waving goodbye to Hunter and Ellie I started to make my way over to my mom and dad who along with Melinda, Henry and Jefferson were talking to Mayor and Mrs. Garrison. Almost having reached them, Grady Michaels' voice came booming over the loudspeaker. He was the Elementary school Principal and had been the MC of the fayre for as long as I could remember. Apart from the one year when he had the mumps and was highly contagious. That year Jim Wickerson did it and got so high on pot laced brownies a couple of the High School seniors gave him, he announced Audrey Montgomery, who ran the dry-cleaning store, as winner of best cow in show—there wasn't even a competition for best cow.

"Ladies and gentlemen, welcome to Dayton Valley Fayre," Grady's voice boomed out. "I'm sure we're going to have another tremendous day, raising money this year for the Sunny Years Old People's Center. We have the usual rides and stalls, and this year we have a dunking booth too. Over by the Haunted House, the lovely Delaney twins are waiting for you to hit the target and drop them into the water. It's just a dollar fifty a throw, so get on over there and give the ladies your money."

I started to giggle imagining Aunt J and Aunt L sitting in bathing costumes and waiting to be dropped into a tank of cold water. They were the only two ladies over sixty who I could imagine pulling it off.

"Also, don't forget," Grady continued, "get your votes in for the Dayton Valley's Easter Queen. We'll be crowning her later, so you don't want your favorite to miss out."

"Huh," I grumbled to myself. "Outdated cliched competition if ever there was one."

"Honey." My mom had spotted me and was waving enthusiastically. "You not having Benny's burrito?"

"No, Mom," I replied through a gritted smile. "Not that hungry."

"You feeling okay?" she asked, running a hand down my arm.

"I'm fine, Mom. Just fine." I turned to look around the field and spotted Carter talking to a girl who I thought worked at the bank. She was younger than me and was gazing up at the damn redhead like he'd just put a glass slipper on her foot and promised her a kingdom.

"That's good," Dad said, pulling me to his side. "We're going to see if we can't dunk Janice-Ann and Lynn-Ann, isn't that right?"

"Sure is." Jefferson dragged his hand through his amazing hair and grinned. "If they want to get dunked then that's what I intend to do, so get your throwing arm ready, honey."

Giving him a small smile, I nodded and followed him and my parents, rolling my eyes at the number of women who were ogling Jefferson—some were even with their partners. God dammit that man was popular. Even my little brother said he was *steezy*, whatever the hell that meant. I could see the attraction. He was tall, muscular, tattooed, his butt looked damned good in a pair of jeans, and every woman over the age of thirty in Dayton Valley was desperate for him. If only Carter wanted me as much.

***

Almost two hours later and I hadn't managed to escape back home. Dad had kept a tight hold of my hand and if he let it go, Mom took over. It was as if they knew I was going to run but were determined that I stay and get used to seeing Carter with other people. Not that I had seen him, except for in the distance and each time he'd been in the company of a woman, or multiple women. Once the Easter Queen was announced I was most definitely escaping back to the security of my bedroom and curling up with a book. Okay, so I'd never read a full book in my life but wasn't that what heartbroken women did—lost themselves in a romance novel and a sexy book boyfriend?

"Okay," Mom said excitedly. "It's time for the Easter Queen announcement. I do love this part."

Dad smiled lovingly at her. "You still got your sash, honey?"

"God, yeah," Henry cried, pointing at Mom. "It was just after college."

"Oh, I remember," Melinda added. "I'd just moved here and thought you were like some fairy princess in that pink chiffon dress you wore. I wanted to be your friend the minute I saw you and asked Sondra to introduce us."

Jefferson chuckled. "I do recall you both got disgustingly drunk that day."

"Yeah, well," Melinda replied, rolling eyes. "I think I was nervous, being new in town and all, and the whole of the town actually being here. As for Sondra, well she just wanted to keep me company in the beer tent."

"Crazy days." Mom sighed and gazed at Dad. "Winning that day was better than when I won Miss Congeniality at Galveston Beauty Pageant."

A look passed between my parents and I knew something big had happened that day but really wasn't sure I wanted to know. I had a feeling it might involve sex and that thought just made me want to puke in my mouth.

"Anyway," Dad said, clearing his throat. "It was the biggest win ever. Did you know that sweetheart?"

I laughed. "Yeah, Dad. You told me."

Mom slapped at dad's arm. "Jim, must you bore the kids with that story every year."

"Yes, because I'm proud of you." He sighed, a happy smile on his face and my heart jumped at the thought that they were most definitely getting back on track.

"Is that why you're so desperate to watch this, Mom?" I asked. "To check no one beats your record."

Mom grinned and glanced between Dad and their friends. "Let's get over there. I think we can push to the front, come on, honey."

The men paved the way for us, moving people to one side with Dad actually saying, "Lady with a baby, coming through," at one point, which earned him a poke from me. Finally, we were right in front of the stage that had been set up in the middle of the field. Hunter and Ellie were there, as were Alaska, Jennifer and Minnesota who we were supposed to have spent the day with. I was surprised to see Nancy Andrews amongst them and what was more surprising was that she was holding onto Minnesota's hand—so the aunts had been right.

"Where did you get to?" Ellie asked, leaving Hunter's side and coming to me. "Every time I saw you, you disappeared. Why didn't you spend the day with us? We've had loads of fun."

"Me too," I replied truthfully, because I truly had.

It'd been nice spending time with the older folks, even though we'd spent far too much time and money trying to dunk the Delaney twins. The in jokes and banter that only lifelong friendships could get away with, had been entertaining to be around. It had also been good to witness Mom and Dad enjoying each other's company.

"Not sure I'm looking forward to this, though." I nodded toward Talia who was standing just two steps away from the stage. "I don't want to watch *her* being crowned."

Ellie shrugged. "She may not."

"I think she may, there's no competition."

We both looked over to see that Talia was the only person standing with Grady, as she looked expectantly at the sash and crown.

"It's so annoying," I huffed. "I really wanted to make it a hat trick of wins before retiring."

"Oh my God," Ellie cried. "I'd forgotten that you'd won it twice before. But you don't have to retire. There's always next year."

"What? No way. How the hell can I run for Easter Queen with stretch marks, saggy titties and bags under my eyes from lack of sleep?" I shook my head. "Nope, the Easter Queen does not come complete with nipple pads, a stroller and baby puke on her shirt."

"You really are an idiot." Ellie rolled her eyes and then turned to the stage. "Oh, God, they're about to announce it. This is so exciting."

I looked at her and frowned. Since when had Ellie been so interested in the Easter Queen?

As Ellie clapped and bounced excitedly, Hunter grinned and pulled her against his side, kissing her temple. Seeing them wind themselves around each other, helped my spirits rise. At least my best friend was getting the man she deserved and loved. All I could hope was that Carter and I remained friends for the baby's sake.

"Okay, ladies and gentlemen," Grady called over the microphone. "It's time to announce your Easter Queen."

Talia took a step forward and started to wave regally at the crowd and it took all my effort not to puke.

"I'm not sure I can watch this," I whispered to Ellie.

"Stay," she hissed back. "Be the better person."

With a shake of my head and a sigh, I kept my spot beside her and waited for Talia's name to be called out.

"With the biggest vote we've ever had," Grady continued. "I can happily say…"

"Oh no, someone broke my mom's record," I gasped.

"Shush," Ellie replied. "Just listen."

"I can happily say that with nine thousand and twenty votes, our winner this year is…" The unified sound of all the spectators inhaling with expectation combined with the drum roll of the town band. "Bronte Jackson."

There were cheers and squeals as Ellie pulled me into her side, only for me to then be dragged from her arms into Dad's so he and Mom could smother me with kisses. Jefferson and Hunter shouted their congratulations and Alaska began chanting my name, while Henry and Melinda whooped. I was hugged and kissed and couldn't quite believe I'd won. It was a small town, dated, cliched contest but I was overjoyed to have won it.

"Bronte," Grady finally called. "Please come up to the stage."

The crowd parted and I made my way to Grady, ready to receive my sash and crown. Totally shocked but undeniably elated.

"Congratulations, Bronte." Grady said as he hugged me. "A huge vote. And congratulations to your runner up, with the other two votes…"

I turned and flashed a false smile at Talia, not caring that I was being a sore winner.

"Mrs. Callahan."

The crowd gasped collectively, and Mrs. Callahan stepped on the stage next to me while Talia turned and pushed away through the onlookers.

"Well done, Mrs. Callahan," I said, giving her a hand a squeeze.

"Yeah, well," she replied, giving a half-smile. "If damn Carter Maples hadn't been your campaign manager, I reckon I'd have had it."

I took a step back wondering what she was talking about.

"Every damn time I've turned around in the grocery store, the library, Delphine's, even in the ladies' section of Myrtle's department store, there he was asking people to vote for you."

"He did?"

"Yeah, he damn well did. You ever tried to buy lube with Carter looking over your shoulder asking you to 'vote Bronte'. Even got anyone with kids to promise their kid's vote too." Mrs. Callahan shoved out her hand and looked down at it. "So, I guess congratulations are in order."

We shook hands and as we did, Mayor Garrison stepped forward with my crown and sash, then loud and clear I heard a voice I knew well.

"Yes, yes. Go Lollipop." He was jumping and fist pumping the air. "Love you, baby. Love you so fucking much."

It was then I burst into tears and leaving the Mayor holding a purple velvet cushion, ran as fast as I could towards my man.

CHAPTER 23

Carter

A s the beautiful blue haired girl came bounding towards me, I braced myself. I'd done good. Yes, indeed I had.

"Oh my God,' Bronte squealed as she launched herself into my arms. "I love you, so much."

Wrapping her legs around my waist, she peppered my face with kisses. Something clicked inside my chest, like I'd found that missing puzzle piece, the one that had been hidden under the sofa for a couple of weeks and then suddenly appeared again.

"Lollipop, I'm so glad you came out from under the sofa."

She paused from kissing me and stared. "What?"

"Ah fuck it, it doesn't matter."

My lips were on hers and nothing or nobody existed around us. It was just me and my Lollipop reconnecting, showing everyone that what we had was right and was meant to be. My hands slipped under her shirt, or should

I say my shirt—I'd recognized it the minute I'd seen her, and it'd given me hope that she was most definitely thawing toward me. So, thanking every God there was, I held her close. I wasn't letting her go ever again, no matter what those crazy hormones did.

Pushing her body to mine, Bronte's legs and arms wound tighter and my dick jerked. It had been too long, and I was more than ready to get her screaming my name. Fuck trying to prove we were more than just sex. As for my dick, well that was most definitely more than ready to be in on the action. Both of us began to breathe heavily, hands and tongues taking what was needed.

"Um, honey, I think you need to go get your crown and sash."

Darcy's voice sounded between us, but I couldn't pull away from the beautiful woman in my arms.

"*Bronte*," Darcy urged. "They haven't finished the crowning, honey."

It was Lollipop who broke our connection, but she did so with a groan, leaning her forehead against mine.

"I need to go finish being made queen," she whispered.

"Yeah, I guess you do."

I slowly dropped her to the floor and gave her one last kiss to the end of her nose. "Go get your crown, sweetheart."

With a huge smile and giggle she extracted herself from my arms and ran back to Grady and Mayor Garrison. I was proud of her and every minute I'd spent haranguing the folks of Dayton Valley to vote for her had been worth it.

"You owe me," Hunter said into my ear. "Two hours I had to sit with Mabel Clooney. Two hours of drinking her piss weak coffee and listening to tales of her 'wonderful Jennings'. You know that son of hers leads a damn boring life in Portland. How many grave rubbings can one man get? Not least the fact it's a fucking weird hobby."

Okay, so Hunter had helped get Bronte some of those votes.

"Yeah," I breathed out. "I owe you."

Fact was I'd give anyone anything. I had my woman back—best feeling in the damn world.

***

"Please, Carter," Bronte gasped as my lips grazed her hip bone. "I need you so much baby. I need you inside me, like… oh my God, now."

My tongue followed the path my lips had taken, enticing and teasing, lifting her to the peak of pleasure. And as she squirmed and stretched underneath me, my dick ached to be inside of her, but I wanted to prolong the desire and prolong the need.

"Don't ever leave me again," I whispered against the roundness of her stomach. "Know that I love you, will always love you, no matter what."

"I know. I know." Her head thrashed from side to side as my fingers trailed up the inside of her leg and traced patterns on her smooth skin. "Carter."

She arched her back, pushing her hips forward, urging me to be inside of her, whether it was with my fingers or my dick, I don't think she cared. I got her though, I understood her need.

Sitting back, I placed a hand on each of her knees and parted her legs, looking down at her wet pussy. It was beautiful and pink, her blonde pubic hair a thin, neat strip framing it to perfection. How the hell I'd managed to last all those weeks without her, I had no clue.

"Gonna rock your world now, Lollipop."

"Yes. Oh God, yes."

Unable to wait any longer, I pushed inside of my beautiful girl and groaned with pleasure as the sensation ripped from my balls and shot up my spine before spreading around my body like ripples in a pond. Each single thrust heightened the want, increased the gratification and compounded my love for her.

Fingertips dug into my shoulder and back as Bronte's hips pushed and pulled in time with mine. She gave, I took, I gave, and she took. We were in perfect synchronization. We were born to fit together. Made to love one another.

"Harder," Bronte panted against my ear.

"The baby?" I questioned, pausing for a moment but starting my rhythm again as soon as Bronte squeezed her legs around my waist.

"It's fine. Nothing will hurt it."

I gave her what she needed and went harder. Keeping one hand on her waist and grabbing hold of the headboard with the other, using it to anchor me inside of her as my thrusts got faster and firmer.

"*Carter.*"

Bronte's ultimate cry was loud and keening, echoing around the bedroom as everything increased—the speed, the desire, the moans and passion.

"Fuck," I groaned as the spark inside of me ignited into a ball of fire and I came with a roar. "*Lollipop.*"

Both my hands grabbed the headboard and I held on tight, wringing out every last drop of cum and pushing as far as I could inside of her. Staring down at Bronte, my heart felt like it was going to beat right out of my chest. Her lips pouted and blue eyes blinked slowly.

"Oh my God, I needed that," she whispered as she reached up and dropped a sweet kiss to the end of my nose. "I missed you, baby."

"I missed you too. More than you will ever know." I wrapped my arms around her and rolled us so that I was on my back and Bronte was lying on my chest, right where she was meant to be. "You think everyone will be pissed that we just split on them?"

She looked up at me and grinned. "I doubt it. They just want us to be happy and I think they all know that this is where we're happiest."

"Yeah, I guess so." My smile showed her there was no guessing about it. I knew so, for definite. "We good now?"

She nodded and I framed her face with my hands.

"I need the words, Lollipop. You have to know I can't go through that again, being without you. For me, this that just happened, means we're back on track. We do this together and we talk about you moving in. You with me on that?"

I needed to nail everything down. There could be no more questions or misunderstandings and our future had to be planned; me, Lollipop and the baby.

Bronte shifted in my arms and rested her chin on my chest, running a finger along my bottom lip. "Most definitely we're good and we can talk about me moving in."

"Good to know. So, let's talk." I was an impatient man where she was concerned, that was for sure.

"Okay, but first there's something I need to do."

She licked her lips and my dick twitched, ready for round two. The hormones had made her insatiable, but I was pretty sure I could keep up, no problem.

"Yeah, and what's that?" I asked, reaching up to kiss her softly.

Instantly she was pushing up and dragging herself away from me. "I really need to eat, like right now. I'm starving."

Before I had a chance to question, or argue, Bronte was disappearing through the bedroom door, giving me a great view of her heart-shaped ass. So, smiling to myself, I pushed out of bed and followed her into the kitchen, knowing I'd follow her anywhere she damn well wanted to go.

CHAPTER 24

Bronte

Ellie looked absolutely joyful and so very much in love as she held out her hand. Hunter had asked her to marry him a few days before and of course she'd said yes. They were meant for each other, better suited than any other couple I knew. The absolutely kick ass, pear shaped diamond he'd presented her with, while on one knee, down by the creek on his pop's land had to have helped too. It was beautiful and everything Ellie had done for the last hour at their impromptu engagement party at Stars & Stripes had been done with a flourish of her left hand.

I was happy for them. For myself not so much. Carter and I had been back together a little under a month and it had been amazing. Lots of sex, lots of cuddling and whispering into the night about our baby, more sex and just a whole lot of fun. My problem was me, or my body to be exact. I was excited about the baby, I really was, but what it was doing to my body was not so good.

Baby Maples—yeah it was getting Carter's name, I wasn't a modern woman who wanted it to be double barreled. Aside from Jackson-Maples being a mouthful and sounding like an old time Motown Singer, my experience of people with double barreled names was they were dicks—in my humble opinion. Anyway, the fact of the matter was Baby Maples had had a growth spurt and I was now at a point where I really couldn't tie the laces of my sneakers. Carter took great delight in having to do them every morning, because yes, heels were getting to be a challenge too.

I'd practically moved into his apartment, bar a few items of clothing and personal items still at home, even though it hadn't been done officially. There'd been no big goodbye to my folks and my childhood home, I'd simply stayed at Carter's most nights and gradually filled his drawers with my stuff. I liked it that way. Carter and I weren't really big on grand gestures, him arranging for me to win Easter Queen aside. We just liked to get on with things. I was pretty sure if he ever asked me to marry him it'd be in a bar in Vegas when we were both drunk on Whisky Sours. An hour later we'd be married. That would suit me just fine. I was girly and loved everything pink, but I'd never wanted a big wedding, not the sort that Ellie had dreamed of from the minute we'd seen pictures of Prince Charles and Lady Diana's wedding in our British History class. Ellie looked like the heart eyed emoji as Miss Bambucci told us all about what a huge occasion it had been. Me, I thought it a little over the top and the dress had needed a press, but what did I know?

"Okay," Carter said with a small smile. "One coke."

Sighing, I pushed it back to him. "I'm not drinking coke. I told you that."

"When?" he cried. "When did you tell me that?"

"Like, an hour before we came out."

Carter laughed and I narrowed my eyes on him. "An hour before we came out, I was inside you, Lollipop. So, forgive me if I don't quite remember what you said while I took you to the fucking moon and back."

I glanced over at our parents who were sitting at the next table along. "Carter my folks might hear."

"They're drunk and the music is loud there's no way they heard me."

I leaned forward and poked Jennifer's arm. She, Alaska, Minnesota, Nancy, Shaw and Austen were at our table—and yes there was still a war going on between Shaw and Nancy, tonight it was a cold one while they ignored each other.

"Jennifer, did you hear what Carter just said to me?" I asked as she looked my way and smiled.

"No, honey. Why, was I supposed to?"

Carter let out a low laugh, while I sighed. "No, it's fine."

"See. No one heard. Now, tell me if you don't want coke, what do you want?"

"Well, what did you get me last time?" I arched a brow and stared him down.

"I didn't. You took yourself a complimentary orange juice from Penny when we came in. Seeing as you've made that last a hella long time, you're going to have to help me out here, Lollipop."

Ugh, why did he always have to be right about everything?

"Apple juice," I snapped back.

"Okay. Now, that wasn't so difficult was it." He leaned in, pecked a kiss to my lips and then disappeared back to the bar.

"You coming to dance?" Jennifer asked as she and Alaska stood up.

I shook my head. "Maybe later."

"You okay, sis?" Shaw called over the music. "You usually love to dance."

"Yeah, well," I replied, pointing down at the bump stretching the fabric of my red dress. "I'm not usually carrying another human onto the dancefloor with me."

"You're getting plenty of exercise though?" Nancy asked as Minnesota stroked a hand down her long hair, his eyes firmly on her bare shoulder.

Shaw's head almost swiveled off his neck. "You train to be a nurse in the last few months or something?"

"I work at a school where two of the teachers are currently pregnant. I listen to that shit all day." Nancy held her hand up to me. "No offense, Bronte. I'm not saying your baby is shit, just hearing all the details all day every day is a bit…"

"Boring," Minnesota finished for her, pulling his blond hair back from his face. He and his brother were good looking men, and he and Nancy were a really handsome couple, I could see why they'd been attracted to each other.

"No, I didn't mean that," Nancy continued as she nudged him in the side. "I was just trying to point out to Mr. Lawyer Man here that I heard exercise is good for Mom and baby."

"Well," Shaw said tilting his head and taking a tone like he may well be talking to a baby. "Mr. Lawyer Man here thinks Miss. Teacher Aide should just butt out of his private conversations with his sister."

Nancy narrowed her eyes and I saw her hand fist on top of the table. I was pretty sure Mr. Lawyer Man was about to get banked on by Miss. Teacher Aide. Minnesota obviously saw it too because he stood and dragged Nancy up with him.

"Come on, tiger, I think we need to dance."

Once they'd left the table Austen blew out a breath. "Oh man, you so want to tap that."

Shaw and I turned to him both of us wide-eyed. I mean, I was pretty sure he was right—they were just like Carter and I used to be for goodness' sake—but… tap that?

"Austen, where the hell did you hear stuff like that?" I asked, pulling at the hairs on his arms, at the same time as wondering when the hell did *they* happen?

"Hey, that hurt and I'm fifteen," he cried, throwing his hands into the air. "When will you people realize I'm not a little kid any longer."

"You're fourteen," Shaw and I chorused.

"Ah whatever, I'm going to find somewhere else to sit. You guys cramp my style anyway." The almost six feet tall kid, not quite a man whose hormones were kicking in, pushed back his chair and stormed off to sit with our parents.

"*We* cramp his style," Shaw said. "He's gone to sit with the old folks."

I shrugged. "Tell me about it."

"Tell you about what?" Carter was back standing at my side as he placed an apple juice in front of me.

"Austen," Shaw replied. "He thinks the 'rents are cooler than us."

We all looked across to see Jefferson, dressed in a three-piece suit minus the jacket with his shirt sleeves rolled up to display his tats, a thick, heavy watch on one wrist and some leather bracelets on the other, making Austen laugh about something.

Collectively we sighed, realizing our little brother was right. Jefferson was way more *steezy* than anyone.

"Oh hey," Shaw said suddenly, pushing up from his chair. "Food is out."

"You want some?" Carter asked turning to go.

"I can carry a plate, Carter." He inhaled and I was pretty sure I saw his mouth move. "Are you counting to ten?"

"No, Lollipop," he replied a little too breezily. "Not at all. Now, while I realize you're more than capable of carrying a plate, I figured to save time in the line and to allow you to chat with my sister who is coming over here, I'd go get you a plate. That sound good?"

It was all said through gritted teeth.

"I can't help being a bitch you know," I spat back. "I don't wake up each morning and make a conscious decision about it."

"I know," he said a little softer. "Which is why I'm trying real hard here and remembering how fucking shit it was when we were apart."

"Why do you need to do that?" I asked, feeling a twitch underneath my eye.

Carter smiled and then straightened down his shirt, which, by the way, was a gorgeous dark green slim fit which showed off his flat stomach and great biceps.

"Because, remembering that helps me to realize all this is worth it."

"All what?"

"Okay, Lollipop," he said, kneeling down next to my chair. "You want to tell me what's going on? What's upset you tonight?"

"Hey guys." Ellie arrived at our table and waved—with her left hand.

"Ellie," Carter ground out. "Hunter let go of you at last."

Ellie coyly lifted a shoulder and rubbed her cheek against it, a move I'd never seen her do before. It was cute but a little cringey all at the same time.

God, why was I being so hateful?

"Yeah, he's talking to Jacob Crowne. Hey," she said moving closer, "did you know Lydia had an affair?"

"No way," I gasped. "I just thought they'd grown apart."

Carter got to his feet and placed a hand on my shoulder. "You want me to get you some food or not?"

I huffed out a sigh. "I don't know Carter, do I?"

"I have no clue, Bronte," he said, throwing his hands into the air. "Because everything I've done tonight, except fuck you into unconsciousness has been wrong. So, you tell me."

"Carter," Ellie admonished. "She's pregnant."

"You don't need to tell me, Ellie," he retorted, putting his hands to his hips. "I've been suffering for it all damn evening."

His words felt like a slap to the face and without warning the tears started to fall. Silently at first, but once I saw Carter close his eyes and pinch the bridge of his nose, the sobbing and donkey noises started.

"It's not fair," I brayed. "You have no idea what it's like. Do you have to carry a beach ball under your clothes every day? No, you don't. Do you have gas coming out of both ends no matter what you eat? No, you... okay yes you do, but that's different." I sniffed loudly and let out a snort. "I can't even paint my toenails, or drink wine and I've eaten so many canned peaches I hate them now and they used to be my favorite."

"If it helps, I still *love* your watermelon sugar," he replied, wiggling his brows. "So, at least one of us getting our portion of daily fruit."

As I let out another loud wail, Ellie rushed to my side, shoving Carter out of the way.

"Lollipop," he sighed.

"It's your fault," Ellie snapped. "You couldn't keep that thing of yours to yourself could you. Hey, Bronte, ignore him he's just a stupid ginger idiot."

"But I love his hair," I howled.

"Ellie move, let me talk to her," Carter growled.

"No," I cried. "I want Ellie."

Carter shook his head and throwing his hands into the air stormed away, which only went to ramp up my weeping and wailing to a higher level.

***

Twenty minutes later and I had finally stopped crying. Mom and Ellie had taken me to the bathroom, where I'd insisted on being left alone. Having touched up my makeup and blown my nose, I wasn't quite ready to go back into the party. There was too much happiness in there. Ellie looked too gorgeous in her tight, cream-colored dress with cute little capped sleeves and sexy rose-gold sandals on her feet.

"Oh God, I'm such a bitch," I groaned, and the tears threatened to start again.

As I was sitting on the toilet seat, I grabbed a handful of toilet tissue and wiped my nose before dropping my head into my hands. Lost in my misery, I didn't hear the bathroom door open, or hear the footsteps on the black and white tiles.

"Hey, Lollipop."

I looked up to see Carter's gorgeous smile and my heart stuttered.

"I'm sorry," I squeaked out.

He reached out and ran a finger down my cheek. "Don't worry about it. It's not a problem." He crouched down beside me and took a hold of my hand and squeezed it.

"I thought you hated me."

He laughed quietly. "Never gonna happen."

"But you walked out on me because you were mad."

Shifting his position so he sat on the floor—I was grateful for Penny's almost anal cleanliness of her bathrooms—he moved in front of me and crossed his legs. He then reached for my foot and lifted it into his lap.

"What are you doing?" I asked through a shaky giggle.

Looking up at me through his lashes, he smiled and winked before removing my shoe.

"Carter?"

"You said you couldn't paint your toenails, right?" I nodded and he reached into his pants pocket and produced a bottle of bright pink nail polish. "So, I'm going to do them for you."

I had never felt so much love inside my chest. Too much. I was in danger of my heart combusting. He smoothed his hand over my foot and then unscrewed the cap of the polish.

"I could have asked Lilah you know," I said, leaning down so our heads were inches from each other.

With a brilliant smile he said, "Yeah I know, but I wanted to do it."

"You didn't walk out on me?"

"No, Lollipop," he said focusing on getting the right amount of polish on the brush. "I went home to get this."

With the tip of his tongue poking out from his lips, Carter made the first sweep onto my pinky toenail. He then sat back, examined it, using his nail to scrape away a little bit of the polish that had touched the skin. Once he was happy, he put the brush back into the bottle and then moved onto the next toe.

"Carter," I said softly.

"Yeah, Lollipop?" he asked without looking up.

"I love you, baby."

Then I got the eyes and the smile.

"Love you too."

He squeezed my foot gently and then went back to work.

CHAPTER 25

Carter

“**I** think our boy is by far the most handsome, don't you?”

Bronte smiled and rolled her eyes. “He is baby, but you have to stop telling the other moms and dads.”

I looked around at the other couples with their dogs of varying age and size and shook my head.

“Nope. Not possible not to boast about Mani. Look at him.” We both looked down at Mani who was happily chewing the end of his tail. “He's damn handsome.”

He'd grown a lot in the month or so that Bronte had been living in the apartment. Mainly outward and I had to keep telling her to stop with the treats. It would not look good to see the local vet carrying around his pup because it was too fat to walk.

“I have to admit,” Bronte whispered into my ear. “He's the most well behaved here.”

"True." I leaned down and rubbed Mani's ear, earning a little grunt from him. He hated to be disturbed when he was chowing down on his tail. "Look at that one over there, with the big woman and her tiny husband. It's crazy."

The large woman was wearing a pair of tailored shorts and a Hawaiian shirt that looked like it might fit her, her husband and any kids they might have. The husband on the other hand was small, balding and wearing mirrored shades. His pants and shirt, in matching khaki, looked like they might be polyester, and in the mini heatwave we were having you could most likely fry an egg on that bald head of his. As for their pooch, well he had them both tied up with his leash as he weaved in and out of their legs, only stopping every few seconds to howl.

"It's probably worried his owner is going to die of heatstroke," Bronte giggled. "He's sweating like a whore in church on Sunday."

"And maybe *he's* worried his wife is going to suggest sex when they get home and," I said with a smirk, "she likes to be on top. I reckon the guy is scared as all get out."

Bronte leaned into me, laughing, and I dropped a kiss to the top of her head. She'd been feeling much better the last few weeks, embracing the changes to her body and feeling calmer about everything. We were coming up to the final trimester and getting more excited each day about the new arrival. We'd decided not to find out the sex of the baby mainly because I'd not been able to make the sonogram where Dr. 'Hollywood Smile' Baskin was going to tell us. I'd been stuck doing an emergency operation on the twisted gut of an Irish Wolfhound and so Bronte has asked not to be told. After that, we agreed that it was kinda more exciting to be surprised on the day. Didn't stop me thinking though, and I was still convinced it was a boy—I'd definitely seen a Johnson on that first sonogram.

"Are we ready, everyone?" A tall guy, with a mop of black hair that fell to his shoulders, beckoned us all toward him. "Please make a circle around me."

We all did as we were told, some dogs making it easier for their owners than others. Mani, however, was a star in the making and trotted alongside me, glancing up every few seconds as if to say, 'look how great I am, Dad'.

"I'm Dwayne your instructor as you know, because you wouldn't be here otherwise." He looked down to the floor and I was sure he was pausing for applause. When none came, he carried on. "So, first things first, I'd like you to introduce yourself and your dog and tell me what you want to achieve from these sessions." He pointed at a young couple around our age, who had a tiny little terrier.

The guy cleared his throat. "I'm Jeff and this is my wife, Hannah. We're here with Buttercup because she won't come back if we let her off the leash."

"No damn wonder," Bronte whispered. "Who'd want to be saddled with a name like Buttercup. Poor dog's probably hoping for a new home and identity."

I snorted out a laugh, earning a glare from Dwayne.

"Would you like to go next?" he asked, giving me a tight smile.

"Sure," I replied and pushed Bronte forward. "You're up, Lollipop."

Stumbling forward, she glared at me over her shoulder. "You do it."

"No, you're the one who wanted to drive twenty miles out of town when I told you I could train him." I winked and flashed my 'I'm gonna eat you out later' smile, because she looked so damn sexy. I obviously knew my girl well because she let out a breath and caught her bottom lip between her teeth.

"Hi," she said, quickly turning back to the group. "I'm Bronte and this is Carter." She then bent to scruff Mani's ears and as if he knew she couldn't bend too far, he stretched up to meet her. "This is our little guy, Mani." She smooched his nose with her own. "He's so beautiful, yes he is."

Dwayne held up his hand. "Let me stop you there, Bronwyn."

"Bronte," she corrected.

Ignoring the correction, Dwayne carried on. "I don't know what your specific issues are with Mani, but I'd say they stem from you talking to him like he's a baby."

"But he is," Bronte protested.

"He's a puppy." Introductions forgotten because we were seemingly *the* worst pupils ever; Dwayne addressed the rest of the circle. "That's a classic mistake thinking your dog, your puppy, is your child. You are the master. The pack leader, not their parent."

"Well fuck me," I muttered leaning closer to Bronte. "I know you said he had a reputation for being good, but was that as a dog trainer or a dictator?"

"I'm beginning to wonder," Bronte hissed from the side of her mouth. "I think I already hate him."

If we hadn't paid for the ten sessions up front, I might have been tempted to take my woman and my dog and just leave. Let's say it was a wonder he hadn't broken his arm patting himself on the back, he was *that* good according to his own endorsement on his website. And, of course, he charged prices that matched the reputation he'd given himself.

"Have you thought of having an actual child?" Dwayne asked, steepling his fingers under his chin, as he addressed Bronte again. "Instead of a dog substitute."

I bust out a laugh as she gasped. She was wearing shorts and a tank with my shirt, unbuttoned, over the top, but there was no disguising she'd got one in the chute—damn her fucking glorious tits were evidence enough.

"What the hell do you think this is?" Bronte cried, pointing at her stomach. "Gas?"

Mani, sensing his momma was getting a little agitated, stood and did a little growl.

"Hey, Mani, it's okay," I soothed, bending to rub his head.

"Ah you see," Dwayne said pointing at me. "Another mistake. Telling him it's okay to be angry."

Getting to my full height I crossed my arms over my chest. "He knows Bronte is feeling stressed," I said thinking the money we'd already shelled out no longer mattered. "I was just reassuring him."

At Veterinary school I'd done an evening class on animal behavior to get extra credit, so I was pretty sure I knew my dog, any dog for that fact, better than Dwayne the dick.

"No, no, no. That's wrong."

The guy never knew when to shut the fuck up.

"Excuse me." Bronte stepped forward and by the way her hands were now on her hips, I knew she was ready to blow. "I think Carter knows what he's talking about. He's a vet in Dayton Valley."

Dwayne, unphased by that snippet of information, shrugged. When I heard Bronte growl, I knew for definite that the over inflated price of the training sessions would have to be written off as a bad investment.

"Come on, Lollipop," I said, grabbing hold of her hand. "Let's go."

"I think you're making a big mistake," Dwayne said and pointed at Mani. "That dog will never be trained if you don't see this through and change your attitudes."

I held tight to her hand as Bronte made her move. "Nope, honey. Come on." We began to move away and just before we did, Mani gave a growl and a bark in Dwayne's direction.

"You see," he called after us. "It's wild."

Once we reached my truck, I figured it was finally safe to let go of my hold on Bronte.

"What a douche." She threw her hands into the air. "I am so sorry I said we had to go to him. He has no idea." She stooped down and picked Mani up, even though he was getting way too heavy. "How could he say you're not our baby."

"Okay, Lollipop, he's too big for that. Give him to me." I pulled him into my arms and rubbed his belly before putting him back on the floor.

"I am sorry, baby." Bronte wrapped her arms around me and rested her cheek against my chest. "I thought..."

She trailed off and when she didn't continue, I pulled back to get a better look at her.

"What is it, Lollipop? What did you think?"

Big blue eyes looked up at me through her hair, the blues and pinks were much paler now and had her original blonde mixed in. It was a gorgeous watercolor rainbow framing her beautiful features. There was worry etched there and I couldn't believe that it was all over a dog trainer.

"This isn't just about training Mani, is it?

"What if we can't look after a baby? What if Mani is about as much as we can handle?" She chewed on her bottom lip. "I'm excited and scared to death in equal measures."

The exhale I made was one of relief. My shoulders sagged as I held her closer. "God, I'm so glad you feel the same the way. I thought you had this, that it was just me who felt out of their depth. But you know what," I said, dropping a kiss to her forehead. "I know we'll be good because we're doing it together. In any case, muddling along isn't a bad way to bring up a kid you know."

She laughed softly and let out a long breath, her fingertips pushing into my back. "Poor kid."

Dropping my hand to her stomach, I gave it a gentle rub. "We'll figure it out. This baby is going to be loved, the rest will just follow."

As I went to move my hand something stopped me. Bronte looked up at me and grinned.

"You feel that?" she asked.

"Shit." My eyes went wide as I looked down at Bronte's stomach and willed it to move again. "That's amazing."

"He's been real lazy and should have moved before, maybe a week or so ago. Then I felt something for the first time this morning when you were in the shower."

I took a step back and felt my blood run cold. Ice in my veins. "You told me you felt something two weeks ago. Why did you say that?"

She shrugged and placed her hand on top of mine. "I thought it might be and then when it didn't happen again, I wondered if it was gas. I mentioned it to Dr. Baskin at my last appointment but when he did the sonogram, he said he had a strong heartbeat and was just a little lazy."

"Wait, he said 'he'?"

"Well actually no, he was careful to say 'it'." Curling up on her toes, she kissed me. "But *I* think it might be a boy. I think that super sperm of yours made us a blue one."

"I don't really care, Lollipop." Letting out a shaky breath I hugged her closer. "Whatever, boy or girl, I'm going to love it with all my heart and will spend my life making sure it's safe and protected."

"Oh, baby, I love you."

When my lips met hers, I knew it was going to get hot and heavy pretty quick. I could spend every minute of every day inside her, loving her. Of course, we'd need to eat at some point, but I'd figure it out.

"Let's go home," I whispered against her lips, grinning as I remembered how she'd reacted to my pussy eating smile earlier. "So, I can show you how much I fucking love you."

We pulled apart and I immediately bent down to tell Mani we were going home, but there was no sign of him.

"Shit. Mani, hey boy, where are you?"

Bronte looked at me and panicked. "Oh God, we lost him. I told you we were going to be crappy parents."

Turning around, my eyes searching the parking lot for our puppy I felt huge relief when I spotted him over by a Mini. A Mini with Dwayne Driscoll Dog Trainer decal on the sides. We both started to walk toward him, thankful he hadn't gone far.

"Mani, you're a naughty little puppy," Bronte cooed as we reached him.

"What you doing here?" I asked with a shake of my head. When I reached down to pick up his leash, the smell of shit hit me. "What the fuck."

Bronte started to giggle. "Oh God, Carter, look, he's pooped right under the door."

And there it was, a huge pile of shit, right where Dwayne would probably step in it, considering it was already going dark and he had over an hour of preening left.

"Good boy," I said, roughing him around his ears. "You're so damn clever. Okay, let's go home."

As I picked up the leash, he cocked his leg and pissed up the door, bringing a gasp from Bronte.

"Carter, look," she cried. "He cocked his leg for the first time. He's never done it before. My clever boy."

"See," I replied, taking her hand in mine. "We're fucking brilliant at raising kids. This is going to be as easy as pie."

Then we went home, and I fulfilled the promise I'd made with my smile while Dwayne Driscoll was being a dick.

CHAPTER 26

Bronte

"I'm still not sure about the color, baby." I stood back and tilted my head to one side, looking at the wall that Carter had just painted a pale lemon. "You don't think it's a little wishy-washy?"

He took a deep breath and ground out, "Nope."

I got why he was a little pissy, it was the third time we'd painted the walls of the nursery, which after me living there for two-and-a-bit months, I'd finally agreed we needed to start.

Glancing at the kick ass jungle mural, which Jacob Crowne had created for us, and then back to the walls, my heart sank. "It's not right, baby." Insipid lemon walls just didn't cut it, especially when there was something so awesome on the fourth one.

I saw the paint roller in Carter's hand drop into the tray and then felt the splashes of paint hit my face. That made me feel a tad pissy, but knew I had to keep a lid on it.

"You're mad, aren't you?"

"Nope. So, what color *would* you like."

Yeah, he had his tail up. There was a twitch in his jaw, and I was pretty sure I heard his teeth grind.

"Green maybe." I winced as I said it.

"Would that be the green we used before the cream, which we used before the yellow."

"Lemon, not yellow, baby, but…" I paused wondering whether I should accept the lemon. "We can leave it."

"No. It's fine. You think we can take a break first?"

Time was moving on. It was almost two p.m. and we'd both taken a day off specially to do the painting. If we took a break it wasn't likely we'd get it finished.

"It'll just be a quick one," Carter sighed, obviously reading my mind. "I just need a cold drink."

He looked like he'd run a marathon, he was sweating so much. The AC was barely making any difference because we had the window open for the fumes and Carter had done the majority of the painting, seeing as my beach ball was now more like a yoga ball. This meant I couldn't even bend to reach the paint and if I got on the floor, I couldn't get up again, hence Carter having to work extra hard.

A break was the least he deserved, but I was feeling guilty, so had something better in mind. Something else that would relax him.

Moving over to him, I reached out for his hands and pulled him to me. When we were as close as we could get with a baby between us, I wound my arms around his neck and curled up on my toes to drop a kiss to his lips.

"I'm sorry, baby."

Green paint streaked the ends of his hair falling into his eyes, and there was a cream splash on his cheek. More evidence of how hard he'd worked.

"It's fine," he managed to say before I moved back in for another kiss.

My lips moved along Carter's and my hands ran through his hair, tugging on it, making sure he knew what I wanted. With a quiet moan, he opened up his mouth and invited my tongue in.

"Shit, Lollipop."

I dropped a hand to feel his dick through his sweats. "Thank you for doing this today. I know I've been a pain in your ass."

"Believe me," he sighed. "It's my fucking pleasure."

Breathing heavily, Carter pulled his mouth from mine and slowly turned me around so that my back was to his chest. His arm draped across my stomach and he placed a protective hand over the baby we'd made together. When he took hold of my ponytail, pulling it away from my neck to drop a trail of kisses, a low burn started in my core. Many times, I'd worried whether Carter and I were meant to be parents, if he was ready to settle down, but not once had it crossed my mind that we weren't compatible in the bedroom—or the kitchen, the living room and the bathroom. One tiny touch of his lips, one little stroke from his fingertips had the ability to send me crazy for him.

The hand that had been cradling my stomach, slipped down into the grey sweats that I was wearing—Carter's grey sweats. Fingers moved inside my panties and parted my lips, where I was already soaking.

"Damn."

He pushed inside of me with two fingers and I gasped at the sensation. Every inch of my body was needy for him and whenever Carter gave me what I wanted, I felt like I was on top of the world. When he stroked inside of me, in exactly the right spot, I drew in a shuddering breath, Carter's name on the cusp of the inhale.

Bare against the cotton of my t-shirt, my nipples felt like they were pulsing in time with my heart. Thumping a beat that I was sure Carter could feel and hear.

"Baby," I mewled, moving my head to the side and scraping my teeth along his bicep. My hand moved over the top of Carter's and squeezed it, pushing it against my clit as I chased my orgasm. As the rhythm of his fingers sped up, I pushed my hips forward and held tighter to him.

When his other hand dropped my ponytail and moved to massage my right tit and rub his thumb over my nipple, I felt like I'd been jettisoned into oblivion. Every single part of my body was set alight and the orgasm that exploded through me literally made me see stars.

"So damn easy to get off," Carter whispered against my ear, his fingers still keeping up their steady tempo.

"Only you, baby," I cried through my release. "Only you."

"God, I'm so damn hard," he growled into my ear. "I need to fuck you now."

Without taking any time to think about it, both my and Carter's sweats were pushed down, I was bent over the chair he'd dragged in there for me to rest on, and he was inside me. The pace of his thrusts was punishing, his grip on my hips tight as his fingertips squeezed my skin, but it was pure bliss.

"Yes, baby, yes," I cried. "Faster."

"Fuck you are one sexy little bitch. You damn well love it, don't you?"

Gone was sweet, gentle Carter and dirty talking, hot, Carter had taken his place. He was right. I did love it.

"How hard do you want it? Harder than this?" He sped up and his grip got tighter.

"Yes, yes. Oh shit."

"All damn day you've been enticing me, you know that?" Carter's mouth dropped to my shoulder and nipped it before sucking it, there was no doubt that he'd left a mark. I felt the blood pulsing at the top of my skin. "I fucking love you."

Harder and faster he went and with each stroke I felt another orgasm building. Bigger and so much more even than the last one. When his hand slapped down on my ass, the pleasure it brought once more threw me off the edge of the cliff. Gripping the chair that I was bent over, I pushed against his hips, squeezed my internal muscles and took us both to the pinnacle.

"Fuck."

Carter's cry was loud but when he let go of my hips and stopped drilling into me, I paused momentarily but then continued my own thrusting.

"Fuck no."

"What do you mean 'fuck no'," I cried, glancing over my shoulder. "Keep going. I'm so close, baby."

"No. No. Shit."

There was no movement from him whatsoever. My body had already touched the edges of an orgasm and it wanted to grab the rest of it and howl with pleasure. But, with each second that Carter provided no friction, it slowly slipped away.

"Carter, move. *Now!*"

"I-I-I can't."

Then without any warning, he pulled out of me. I was left holding onto a chair with my bare ass in the air and the fragments of a fucking fantastic orgasm waving goodbye— and believe me when I say it was going to be fantastic, I had no doubt.

"Don't you care," he cried from over my shoulder. "I've got a cramp."

"What?" Pushing into an upright position, I hurriedly and more than a little disgruntled, pulled up my panties and sweats and swung around to face him. "What do you mean you have cramp?"

"What I say. I have a cramp." His face crumpled into a pained grimace as he stretched his leg out. Thrusting both hands to the back of his head, he started to yowl like a Tom cat enjoying a night on the prowl. "Ah shit it hurts so much."

Okay, so I can be a sympathetic person. I can be kind and when Carter had a head cold when we first started dating, I was the perfect nurse. That though was not when I'd just had an awe-inspiring orgasm snatched away from me.

"Oh, for God's sake. Get a damn grip. You do know I'm going to be pushing a baby through my hoo-hah in a little over two months don't you."

"Lollipop, please," he yelled, making a grab for my arm. "You have to help. Aaarrrggghhh."

I took a step back and stared at him. Had he been shot or poisoned or something because there was no damn need for such drama. None at all.

"You for real?" I asked, folding my arms over my still sensitive tits.

"I'm dying here. Don't you care?" He began jumping around with his leg stretched out in front of him.

"Pathetic," I groaned and shook my head, watching on as Carter acted like *he* was the one giving birth.

"Hey there, we let ourselves in with the key Mom gave us. She sent pie."

I turned to see Ellie and Hunter in the doorway. As usual they were touching in some way or other. This time Hunter had his hands on her shoulders, his thumbs rubbing her bare tanned skin.

"Oh wow, when did Jacob put that up."

"Fuck," Carter cried, now tugging at his hair.

"Last night. He called after he picked JJ up from his afterschool club. He's such a cute kid," I enthused as the three of us admired Jacob's work.

"He is, isn't he," Ellie agreed.

"Does that monkey look like Carter, or am seeing things?" Hunter asked, peering closer at the mural.

The three of us leaned closer and began to laugh. Jacob had put Carter's face onto a monkey and when I looked around, I found me too.

"Oh my gosh, there's me."

"Wow, yeah."

"Excuse me," Carter groaned behind us. "Anyone care that I have a cramp. I think I need to go to the emergency room."

We all turned in unison and as we did Ellie squealed and pulled Hunter in front of her.

"For fuck's sake, Carter," Hunter yelled. "You're one dirty fucking douchebag."

"I have a cramp." He was practically sobbing now, reaching out to me with a shaky hand. "Lollipop please."

I sighed heavily and shook my head. "Carter, honey. Please put your dick back in your pants. You're scaring your sister."

CHAPTER 27

Carter

My sister looked at Hunter as though he shit gold nuggets, and as for him, well his eyes had damn diamonds in them when they landed on her.

"Ugh, you two are so sickly," I groaned, taking a sip of the fancy wine that Hunter had insisted on us drinking at the fancy dinner that he and Ellie were springing us.

Bronte slapped at my arm. "Leave them alone. They're in love."

"So are we," I protested. "But I don't slobber all over you all the time."

"Might be nice if you did," she muttered, and I wasn't sure whether she wanted me to hear or not.

"Did I not slobber over you this very morning, Lollipop?" I raised my brows and grinned when she blushed.

"I've seen the way you look at each other and believe me," Ellie said with a roll of her eyes, "you definitely slobber over each other. You just don't realize that's what you're doing."

"After what we saw last week, I'd say there's plenty of loving going on in your apartment." Hunter grinned and winked at me.

Me with my dick out, jumping around in front of my sister, was most definitely something I was going to take shit for. The way Ellie squealed anyone would think she'd never seen a man's Johnson before. I knew for a damn fact that she hadn't lost her cherry to Hunter, so she'd seen at least two before mine. It had all been too fucking dramatic, but that was my sister.

"Anyway," Bronte sighed, forking a tomato from her Cobb salad. "What's with the fancy pants dinner? We could have gone for burgers at the café and saved you some cash."

Ellie rolled her eyes. "You're one ungrateful little brat, you know that, right?"

"It's my natural demeanor," she replied, waving her tomato around. "So, spill it."

Hunter sat up straighter and grinned. "We want to ask you both to be members of the wedding party."

With their hands clasped together on top of the table, they looked between us both. By the look on their faces, you'd have thought they'd just offered us a world cruise on the most luxurious ship on the planet.

"Well, to say I'm underwhelmed is kinda understating it." I rolled my eyes. "I'd have been more shocked if I wasn't going to be your best man."

"And if you ask anyone else to be your head bridesmaid, I'll make sure you change every poopy diaper this baby makes." Bronte ran a hand over her ever-growing stomach and at the sight of it my breath left my lungs pretty quickly.

"You know you look beautiful, Lollipop," I stated and placed my hand on hers.

She smiled softly and I pursed my lips to kiss her when she said, "You think you'll ever get around to asking me to marry you?" The tomato was then popped into her mouth.

Taken a little aback, I looked at Hunter who just shrugged.

"Don't look at me, buddy."

"No, Carter," Bronte said, arching her brows. "Don't look at him."

My attention went back to my pasta as I searched through it for a shrimp. This was not the time or the place, beside which we'd talked about the future many times. It wasn't that she didn't know that I worshipped her. We had a baby on the way for God's sake.

"Are you going to answer me?" Bronte asked. "Or are you going to give that pasta all your attention this evening?"

Putting down my fork, I exhaled and looked up to see three faces looking at me expectantly.

"Lollipop," I sighed. "You know how much I love you. I tell you all the time."

"Saying 'God, Lollipop, I love you, baby', while you're pushing your penis into me isn't quite the same, honey."

"Ugh, please." Ellie took a huge gulp of her wine, shuddered and then looked back to me. "Okay, you can answer now."

"Seriously, Hunt, did you have to bring her along?" Letting out a long breath, I turned back to Bronte. "Don't you think we have enough going on?"

"Oh, what, you mean this?" She pointed at her stomach. "*We* do? Are you sure it's *we*, because I'm the one who has to carry junior Maples around. I'm the one who has to be poked and prodded, I'm the one that has the ankles of my Grammy. *And* I do believe I'm the one that has an ass that could quite easily take up the whole of the east coast. While you, Mr. Carter Maples, Veterinarian, well you don't really have enough going on at all." She held her pointer finger up. "Oops sorry, you do have to save the animals of Dayton Valley, but apart from that..."

Her salad forgotten, Bronte, pushed her bowl away and gave me a sickly-sweet smile, waiting for a response. When I glanced at Hunter and Ellie, they were both leaning with their elbows on the table and staring at us.

"You want me to order popcorn?" I asked.

Hunter waved me away. "No. No, you go for it."

Fucking dickweed.

I turned back to Bronte. "*I* thought *you* had enough to deal with. And, if you recall, Lollipop, up until a couple of months ago, you pretty much told me to get lost. Now, if I suddenly asked you to marry me, I reckoned you might just think I was doing it to tie you to me, or even doing it just because you're cooking my heir in there, not because I want to spend the rest of my life with you." I took her hand and kissed it. "Which I really do. Now, rest assured when I ask you it'll be our kind of beautiful and will come with an awesome ring that'll make that damn rock on Ellie's finger look like a chipping. Okay?"

I sat back, confident that I'd appeased the hormonal craziness that was going on in my true love's head.

How fucking wrong could one idiot man be.

"I asked for commitment, Carter," she cried, her eyes almost popping out of her head. "Don't you think marriage is a tiny way of showing that?"

"Of course, I do," I protested. "But I just explained why I didn't want to suggest that particular level of commitment, yet. And I know you wouldn't want engagement pictures looking fat." I saw darkness shadow her face like a blanket. "Okay, not fat, but pregnant. You know I'm right. I mean you'd want a sexy little dress, high tower heels, cute bag, big hai—

"*Stop.*" She held her hand up to silence me. "Before you really say something that may get you a punch in your balls."

"I don't know," Ellie added. "I think he's said plenty to get him a punch to his tiny little testicles."

"Excuse me," I snapped at my sister. "Those testicles you talk of have produced a baby. And it was the one and only time I went bareback, so I'd say more fucking huge than tiny, thank you, Ellie."

"Someone's a little touchy," Ellie muttered.

Hunter nodded. "His balls are quite tiny though, baby. It's a fucking miracle they produced an offspring to be honest."

"Hunter, man," I growled. "You're getting on my last fucking nerve."

"Just saying." He sat back in his seat and pulled Ellie into his side, kissing the side of her head—damn kiss ass.

"The size of your balls aside, Carter," Bronte continued. "You still haven't answered the original question."

About to answer, by basically repeating myself, I was stopped in my tracks when the waiter came over. He sidled up between Bronte and I and gave that damn creepy smile all waiters give when they're desperate for you to leave them one hell of a tip.

"Everything okay with your meals?" He looked pointedly at Bronte's abandoned salad.

"It's all lovely," Ellie replied and tucked back into her risotto, nudging Hunter to get back to his ribeye.

"Can I get you any more drinks."

Bronte sighed. "Could I get sparkling water please."

He nodded and then looked between the rest of us.

"Another bottle of the wine please," Hunter added.

"Could I get a bourbon and coke." Bronte's gaze snapped to mine. "What?"

"Hunter and Ellie paid for that nice wine and you're drinking hard liquor."

"I kinda feel like I need it, gotta be honest."

The waiter walked away, leaving us in silence. Ellie and Hunter continued eating, not lifting their eyes from their plates. Bronte drummed long pink fingernails on the table, her eyes firmly on me.

"Lollipop, you know I love you." I pinched the bridge of my nose, not entirely sure what more I could say to her. "I only see my life with you in it, make no mistake about that."

"But that won't be with a wedding band on my finger," she replied with resignation.

"No," I disputed. "I don't mean that, at all." I leaned closer to her. "Where's this coming from. You've never once said you wanted to get married before the baby came."

"Doesn't mean because I haven't said it that I don't want it."

The determined jut of her chin told me no matter what I said, she wasn't going to listen or understand. It was stubborn Bronte at her best.

"You said you'd hate the wedding that they're having."

Despite how girly Bronte was, and how Ellie could punch like a guy, their views on the perfect wedding were the total opposite of what you'd expect. Bronte was all for eloping and then having hot sex in a seedy Vegas motel.

"And I would," she replied and turned to Ellie, who had a forkful of food paused at her open mouth. "No offense, Ellie, but the church and big dress thing isn't for me."

"None taken," my sister replied and then shoved her food into her mouth.

Bronte swiveled in her chair, effectively turning her back on Hunter. "I don't want that, but I did think you might have wanted the three of us to all have the same name."

"That's your reason for wanting to be married?" I asked. "Because if it is, it's not romantic."

"Sometimes, Carter you're as dumb as a watermelon." She dropped her head into her hands. "This is ridiculous, you just don't understand where I'm coming from."

"You're right," I replied with a shrug. "I don't." Having managed to snap that last nerve I'd spoken about, I threw my napkin to the table. I then reached for my wallet from my back pocket. "Sorry about this, guys, but I think I'm gonna go."

"Carter, buddy," Hunter protested. "Don't be a dick and just eat your dinner."

I shook my head and threw some cash on the table. I loved the woman next to me with all my damn heart, and would give my life for her, but at that moment I had no damn clue how to deal with her. I'd tried to do everything she'd asked of me—give her space, show her commitment, just generally be the man she deserved, but now she was being downright awkward. I'd already had a shit day, having to put a two-year-old dog to sleep because of an inoperable tumor on its spine. Then I'd had to try and comfort the young couple who'd treated that pup like a kid because they couldn't have children. They were devastated and it had been hard to hold them and myself together. Dinner was the last thing I'd wanted to do but I'd done it because Hunter and my sister invited us, and because Bronte was excited to go out. The conversation though had just damn well soured my already rock-bottom mood.

"Sorry, Hunt, but I'm beat. I've had a real shitty day. That's for the tip." I turned to Bronte. "You coming with me or getting a ride home with Ellie and Hunter?"

Her bottom lip trembled for a second and then she cleared her throat and straightened up. "I'm going to stay and enjoy the rest of my dinner. I'll see you at home later."

Nodding I ran a hand down her hair. "Enjoy the rest of your night."

Waiting outside for my *Uber*, I almost wished I smoked. A cigarette at that point might well have calmed me because, for the first time ever, I wondered whether Bronte and I were ever going to make it.

CHAPTER 28

Bronte

L ying alone in our huge bed, I didn't think I'd ever felt so ashamed of myself. At dinner I'd acted like a totally spoiled bitch. No wonder Carter was passed out cold on the sofa with Mani when I got home.

He was right, if he had asked me to marry him, I'd have always wondered if it was because of the baby. He was also right when he said I wouldn't have wanted any engagement pictures. They'd have to be from the neck up and what would be the point of that. Engagement pictures were almost as important as wedding pictures. They captured that moment when you initially pledged your life to each other; when the girl first knows for certain her man loves her.

I had no clue why I'd been so adamant that we talk about it. I lied, of course I knew why. It was jealousy at Ellie and Hunter's excitement; they were building a house and would soon be planning a wedding. I kind of felt that Carter and I had skipped the important bits, the exciting bits. Not that having a baby wasn't exciting, it was the best thing to ever happen to me, but it made me feel old. We were going to be parents, no longer Carter and Bronte who argued like cat and dog and made up like horny lovebugs. Adulthood had hit us right between the eyes and it scared me.

Throwing the comforter from me, I took a moment to think about what I should say to Carter. How did I apologize, yet make him realize not only was I excited but scared to death about the next phase in our life?

"Ugh," I groaned and slapped my hands over my eyes. "I'm such an idiot."

"Debatable." Gasping, I lowered my hands to see Carter standing over me with a mug in his hand. "Green tea."

Sleepy eyes watched me sit up before he then handed me the steaming drink. I tried to avoid his gaze and let my eyes drop to his torso. There was no doubt about it, he looked damn hot. His plaid pajama bottoms hung low and his chiseled chest was bare, but what I really loved, which I knew made me kind of weird, was the hint of his auburn underarm hair when he placed his hands on his hips. Damn it, I just loved *him* and thought he was so freaking sexy. Which in itself was weird after years of fighting and hating on him. All it had taken to change my mind had been one kiss and some dirty words. He'd told me that he was going to fuck me so good that anyone else that came after him would be a total disappointment.

Boy, had he been right—not that there'd been anyone else since that night. For a while I'd just been addicted to his cock, but quick fucks turned into staying for dinner afterward, which moved on to staying overnight that had then stretched into weekends. And so, within a small window of time, I knew I'd fallen in love with him.

"Can you remember the first time we said the 'L' word?" I asked, wrapping my hands tightly around my mug, feeling comfort in its warmth.

Carter's smile was soft and gentle, with a hint of wickedness as his left eyebrow arched.

"I do and I also remember how I celebrated that fact."

Rolling my eyes, I smiled. I remembered too. I hadn't been able to get into that sort of position as a teenage gymnast, so how the hell I'd managed it ten years later I had no clue.

"We were watching a movie; Romeo & Juliet," I reminded him. "And you really didn't want to."

He shrugged and lowered himself to sit on the edge of the bed. "I thought it was going to be lame."

"I know, but then I saw you crying." My heart did a double bump as I recalled that being the exact moment that I knew. "The fact that the story brought you to tears made me realize that you were so much more than the annoying idiot I'd grown up with."

"Then," Carter said, taking hold of my hand, "you said, 'I love you, baby'. And then you fucking jumped me."

"I did not," I gasped. "I smiled at you and you wiped away a tear and said, 'I love you too'."

"Then you jumped me?"

He said it like it was a question and I couldn't help but laugh. "I think you'll find it was you who jumped me."

"Whoever jumped who it doesn't matter. Amazing orgasms followed." He lifted a hand to take a strand of my hair and run it through his fingers. "A lot of the blue has gone now. You can dye it you know."

"I know. Not sure whether I want to. What do you think?"

He leaned forward and kissed my nose. "You're beautiful either way."

Before he could pull away, I placed my hand on the back of his head and met his gaze. "I'm so sorry for my behavior last night. It wasn't really about getting married, you know that, right?"

Soft lips kissed mine and then a breath whispered over my skin as he sighed.

"What was it about?" he asked, taking the mug from between us and placing it on the nightstand. "I know it's not about a gold band on your finger." He lifted my hand and kissed the exact finger where that band would sit.

"You were really pissed at me, weren't you?"

Carter's head went back, and he exhaled through his nose. I thought he was going to let loose on my ass, but instead when his gaze met mine again, it was with a gorgeous smile. It was full of warmth and love and not for the first time I wondered how the hell I deserved him.

"I was pissed," he replied. "Pissed that it was coming from nowhere and a little pissed that you chose that moment to bring it all up. It was kind of a big deal for Hunt and Ellie, asking us to be in the bridal party."

I gasped because he was right, and I'd been too selfish to realize it. "Oh my God, I feel like such a bitch. I didn't even think about it being their night."

"They paid for a fancy dinner, fancy wine and not just you, but both of us, ruined it for them. I shouldn't have left, but I'd had a real shit day and it was one thing too many."

"Why, what happened?" I edged closer and wound an arm around his waist, loving the feel of warm skin under my fingertips.

"Had to put a young dog to sleep and she was the couple's baby, because they can't have a kid." He looked down at my stomach and smiled but the eyes that met mine were conflicted.

"It's not your fault that they can't have kids, Carter. Or that you had to euthanize their dog."

"I know, but I couldn't help but think." He placed his hands over our baby. "We didn't actually welcome this little one wholeheartedly, did we? We were given this amazing gift, Lollipop and we both acted like a kid that asked for a PlayStation for Christmas and got a coloring book."

"Only for a short time," I offered. "We soon got on board."

"I guess. So, what was last night about? 'Cause, like I said, I know it wasn't about a wedding."

I took a deep breath and placed my hands over Carter's which were still on my belly. "I feel like I've been a real bitch from the moment that little plastic thing told me I was pregnant. I pushed you away because I didn't have faith in you, and that was wrong. Then just as we get back on track I act like a crazy spoiled bitch. Ruining Hunter and Ellie's night too."

"I know what I said, but I do doubt you spoiled their night, Lollipop. They're so wrapped up in each other, and you know Hunter will love the fact that you being pissed at me makes him look good. He's so self-centered he probably didn't even realize what was going on."

I rolled my eyes, knowing that he loved Hunter and that was the only reason he gave him so much shit.

"You know that's not true." I sighed and ran my fingers over his forearm, fascinated to watch his fine hairs stand on end. "He was real quiet after you left. He didn't even eat desert and you know how much he loves pie."

Carter groaned. "If that's an analogy of him and my sister fucking then I no longer want my oatmeal."

"No," I cried, with a smile. "It isn't."

Resting my forehead on his shoulder, I wished that I could turn back the clock to just before we walked into the restaurant the night before.

"Carter," I said without lifting my head. "I'm so sorry. I've turned crazy since I've been pregnant."

"Just a little, Lollipop." He gave a soft laugh and then lifted my head with a finger under my chin. "Tell me."

"I was jealous," I finally admitted. "They're just starting out; new house, wedding, and it feels like we skipped all that bit. Not that the baby isn't exciting, because it is, so exciting. I can't wait for us to be a family, I really can't. I just... well, I worry that we're missing out on so much."

"Jumping ahead to being parents without the excitement of a wedding?"

I shrugged. "Kind of, it's not the wedding, you know that's not what I'm into. I'm scared that we've jumped the important parts and maybe you're only with me for the baby. I'll never know whether you wanted to be with me for me."

Carter chuckled softly and caressed my cheek. "Don't ever think for one moment that I only want you because you're providing me with a child. That is absolutely not the truth. You are the fucking love of my life and okay, so we've moved ahead a little quick, but we're about to enter the most awesome phase of our lives." His lips brushed against mine and I felt tears prick at my lashes. "When I ask you to marry me, it'll be when I know beyond doubt, that you know beyond doubt that I love you more than anything else. When all the crazy hormones have gone, you'll realize your absolute fucking worth, Lollipop. Okay?"

With a single tear rolling down my cheek, I nodded. "Okay."

"Good. Now, you ready for your breakfast?"

"Okay, but I think I'd better call Ellie and apologize first."

Carter waved me away. "Nah, don't fuss it. Hunt's ruined my year, we just spoiled one damn night for him."

"How's he ruined your year?" I asked, brushing his hair from his eyes.

"Marrying my sister. Totally broke the best friend code."

"Like you were ever protective of Ellie," I scoffed.

"God no, it just means now I'm going to have to spend more time with her than ever before. You have any idea how fucking shit that thought is?" He stood and gave me a brief kiss. "Okay, now come on, breakfast is ready."

With a cocky grin, he turned to leave and as I watched his ass, I knew I was the luckiest woman alive.

CHAPTER 29

Carter

We had only six more weeks to go before our lives changed forever. Then baby Maples would arrive. Whether that was a boy or a girl, who knew or cared. I was just about ready to pee myself with the excitement of it all.

Things had been good between me and Bronte in the weeks since she'd freaked out about us not being engaged. Amazing in fact. We were finally free and clear of any insecurities and pretty much ready to become parents.

The shopping trip for the stroller had been something of an experience. Surely a stroller is a stroller? Apparently not. Bronte took almost two fucking hours to decide on something that wasn't too gender specific, too low, too high or too difficult to get into the trunk of her stupid tiny car. It even had to… well, stroll a certain way. I thought she'd decided on one but then the wheels didn't quite turn as she wanted them to. Wheels are wheels, right?

Apart from the stroller, which was at her mom and dad's house, because apparently it was bad luck to have it at our apartment, everything else was ready. All we had to do was relax for the next month and a half. So, we were having our folks over for dinner, because there's nothing more relaxing than organizing that.

"Hey, Lollipop," I called. "You want something to drink?"

She popped her head around our bedroom door. "No thank you. But can you come fasten me up though. I can't reach the zipper."

"Who puts zippers in pregnancy wear?" I replied as I moved down the hall toward her.

"Probably a male designer who's never been pregnant," she complained sulkily.

"So, I kind of have to ask why the hell you bought it?" I followed her into the bedroom and died inside. The room looked like a bunch of toddlers had been in there playing dress-up. There were clothes everywhere, on the bed, on the floor and on the dresser. "Couldn't decide what to wear, hey?"

"I'll clean it all up, I promise. I just couldn't find anything I didn't look fat in."

"You don't look fat," I said, dropping a kiss to the back of her neck as I slowly pulled the zipper up. "You look beautiful."

Bronte sighed contentedly and took my hand, putting it onto her stomach. "I love you for saying it, but I'm seriously fat."

We stood like that for a few seconds, embracing in the silence, when it was broken by Bronte hissing and grabbing my hand tightly over the baby.

"Ah shit." Her fingers clenched mine to the point of pain.

"You okay?" I turned her around to face me. "What's wrong?"

With her eyes closed, Bronte shook her head. "No, I'm fine. It just took me by surprise. I think it was those Braxton Hicks they told us about at the childbirth class.

Blue eyes flicked open and stared at me. There was a hint of tears and I was more than a little worried that Bronte was brushing things off too easily.

"Lollipop, you think we need to call Dr. Baskin?"

She shook her head and loosened her hold on me. "Nope, it's gone now."

Watching her warily, I ran a hand over her stomach but felt no movement of any kind.

"Honestly, Carter, I'm fine. Now go and let me finish getting ready." Giving me a quick kiss, she then moved away to apply some lipstick in the mirror.

She seemed at ease, but I was determined to watch her carefully for the rest of the night.

***

"I don't know why you can't tell us what names you've decided on," Darcy said, sitting back in her seat at our small dining table. "I still like Burlington after Great-Grandpa."

Bronte rolled her eyes. "Mom, I'm not calling a child of mine Burlington." She rubbed her back and I noted that it was the third time she had in the last half hour. "It'll get called Burly or something else just as stupid."

"I always thought James was a good name," Jim offered.

"People might think I'm naming it after Jim Wickerson, or worse Jimmy Foster."

My jaw tightened at the thought of our douchebag fire chief, but I chose to stay silent for once.

"But why, I'm your dad? Of course, you'd be naming it after me," Jim argued.

"Hey, hold your horses," my dad cried. "Other grandpa here."

"Exactly," Bronte sighed. "It'd have to be James-Henry or Henry-James and that's too much of a mouthful, and whose name would go first, and we don't even know if we're having a boy yet."

"You okay?" I asked when I saw her try to hide a wince.

"Hmm. Anyone want more coffee?"

"You sit, honey, I'll get it," Mom said and gave Bronte's arm a rub. "One more cup and then we'll all go."

"It's still early," Dad protested.

"Honey, Bronte needs her rest." Mom got up from the table and squeezed past his chair. It was all a little snug, seeing as we only had room for a small table.

"I'm fine," Bronte protested.

She didn't look fine, I had to be honest. Her face was as pale as the china we'd eaten from and there wasn't much color in her lips either. I leaned into her and placed an arm around her shoulder and as I did, she grimaced again.

"Lollipop, what's wrong. Tell me."

Eyes brimming with tears looked up at me and her bottom lip trembled. "There's something wrong. I'm sure of it. I've been having pain all day, but for the last hour or so it has gotten worse."

Panic kicked me in the gut as I watched a tear roll down her cheek. We were so close, yet too damn far away. The baby couldn't be coming. Not yet, it wasn't time.

"*Mom*," I cried, my eyes still on Bronte. "Call Dr. Baskin and tell him we're going to the hospital. Numbers on the refrigerator. Call Nancy too, she'll take Mani."

"What?" Darcy cried and pushed up from her chair to get to Bronte. "Sweetheart, what's happening?"

"I have so much pain, Momma," she sobbed. "My back hurts and my stomach is hard and keeps tensing and... ah shit. I know I can't be, but I think they're contractions."

Bronte's hand reached out and grabbed my shirt, pulling me to her and screwing the cotton between her fingers.

"Okay, sweetheart. Let's get you out of the chair." Darcy nodded to Jim who had moved to her side with my dad. "You two get her on her feet. Carter, honey, you go get her bag."

"Bag," I repeated. "Bag, where's the bag?"

"My side of the bed. Next to the nightstand," Bronte gritted out.

Scrambling to my feet and almost sending my chair toppling over, I rushed toward the hallway to get to the bedroom. Mom was talking on the phone, pacing up and down while she did. I had never wanted a hug from her so much in all my life. Wasting no time though, I ran into the bedroom and went straight for the small suitcase that Bronte had packed a little over a week ago. I'd given her shit about it being far too early, but she'd insisted. Like she'd had some damn premonition or something.

I grabbed the case and ran back down the hallway, through the kitchen, the living room and then out the door. I started banging on the buttons for the elevator when my door swung open and Dad came out.

"Son, you forget something?"

I looked down at the bag, felt my pocket for my keys and cursed. "No keys. Fuck."

"Well, yeah, you'll need keys," he dangled them in front of me, "but I think you need Bronte too."

"Baby, it hurts so much." Bronte was being helped by Jim and Darcy, while Mom followed close behind with Mani on his leash.

I took the two steps to her and pulled her into my arms. "Okay, Lollipop, it's going to be okay. We'll be at the hospital soon."

"Dr. Baskin will meet you there," Mom said, her voice cracking. "We'll all be right behind you, I texted Nancy and she's okay to take Mani."

At that moment Nancy's door opened and she and Minnesota stepped into the hallway.

"Good luck, buddy." Minnesota slapped my back, while Mom handed over Mani to Nancy.

I looked between everyone gathered outside our apartment and bit my lip to stem the cry of fear that threatened to escape. I had to hold it together for Bronte. She didn't need me losing it, no matter how much I wanted to crumple in a heap of uneasiness.

"Elevator is here, son." Dad got the other side of Bronte and helped me get her into the lift. Once we were in, he held the door open for Darcy to join us, so she could replace him at Bronte's side.

"We'll see you down there." Dad gave me a tight smile and I gave him a chin lift in return as he threw me my keys.

"Okay, sweetheart," Darcy said as the doors closed. "Let's get you to hospital."

"But, Mom, it's too early." Bronte's hand tightened around mine and I guessed there was another pain—a contraction—hitting her.

"That baby will be healthy and strong. It's going to be fine." She glanced at me and though it was quick, I saw the panic in her eyes.

"It's all good, Lollipop," I said. "Everything is all good."

"It's too early right, doc?" I asked as Dr. Baskin led me from the room where he'd left Bronte with Annalise, the Doula we'd been working with at our childbirth classes. Darcy had called her on our way over and seeing her waiting outside for us had been a huge relief.

"It's a little early, yes but baby is definitely coming. There's no getting away from that fact I'm afraid."

Dropping my gaze to the floor, I ran a hand over the back of my head, wondering how the fuck I was going to keep it together. Dr. Baskin placed a hand on my shoulder and gave it a squeeze.

"Baby is a good size, Carter but we may have some respiratory issues. Unfortunately, we won't know until it's here." He led me further away from the door and my stomach lurched, threatening to bring back the dinner Bronte had cooked earlier.

"What is it?" I asked, feeling my legs shake.

"I just want you to be aware that we'll have to take the baby straight away. Annalise is explaining it all to Bronte now, but I think we're going to need you to keep a tight hold of her and keep her calm."

"We can't hold him first?"

"A few minutes but then we'll really need to get the tests done in case treatment is needed. Okay?"

I nodded. "Yeah, okay."

"Good. Now you get in there with Bronte and just act like it's a normal birth, no issues, keeping it nice and calm. Everything is going well, so far all signs are good, so Annalise will beep me when it's time."

With one last tight smile, he walked away leaving me in the hallway feeling out of my depth and with no idea what to do. Looking up and down the hallway, watching out for what I had no fucking clue, I was relieved to see Mom and Darcy approaching me.

"Hey, honey." Mom pulled me into the hug I was desperate for. "You all set?"

She kissed my cheek and then let me go, only for Darcy to drag me into her arms.

"You can both do this," she said softly. "I know my baby girl and she'll be just great."

"I know," I breathed out shakily. "I'm just not so sure I will."

"Honey, you came into this world triumphantly, screaming your lungs out—okay, you were covered in poop, but you were loud and strong. So, of course, you can do this."

"Thanks, Mom." I rolled my eyes and took a step away. "I need to get in there."

"Give her our love," Darcy replied. "And we'll all be waiting. Hunter and Ellie are here too."

Emotion prickled at my throat. Hunter was my best friend and even though I gave her shit, I loved my sister, to have them waiting helped ease my heart a little. As Mom turned to leave, I grabbed her arm.

"Mom, what if—"

She held her hand up and shook her head, biting on a quivering bottom lip. "Not gonna happen, baby. Now go be there for Bronte and bring our grandchild into this world."

When I pushed back into the delivery room, Annalise gave me a bright smile and moved away from Bronte's side.

"Just who she's been asking for." As I passed her, she gave my back a quick rub. "I'll be just over here when you need me."

Placing herself in a chair just away from the bed, I stood in her place and took Bronte's hand in mine.

"You okay. Any pain?"

She nodded with a wince and a little whimper. "It hurts so bad."

Fuck she blew me away. It hurt bad yet all she'd done was a tiny little cry. "You're a warrior, Lollipop, you know that."

Tears rolled down her cheeks and plopped onto her gown. "I'm trying to be brave, for you and the baby, but it's real hard."

Blowing out a breath, I ran a hand down the braid that Annalise had put into her hair. As she looked up at me, I could practically hear my heart beating in my ears.

"I know what I can do."

"What's that?" she asked, through gritted teeth.

I cleared my throat and started to sing. *"When your heart is black and broken. And you need a helping hand..."*

'Ten Storey Love Song' by The Stone Roses was Bronte's favorite song and as I sang it, badly, I finally got a smile from my girl.

CHAPTER 30

Carter

There were no words to describe how I felt about Bronte. I thought I'd loved her before, but to watch her give birth to our son, only determined that the damn woman would own my heart forever. If I could have taken her place and suffered the pain for her, I would have. She was braver and stronger than anyone I'd ever met. No pain relief and the added worry that the baby would be taken from her pretty much straight away, didn't faze her. She dropped her chin, gritted her teeth and was a fucking rock star.

As for my son. My boy. Fuck he was beautiful. He had my eyes and his mom's nose and lips, and I was pretty sure he was going to be a heartbreaker. He was most definitely mine, the attention he was giving to his momma's boobs was testament to that.

"I'm so sorry, honey," Annalise said. "They're going to have to take him now."

Bronte had worried she wouldn't take to motherhood, but she practically growled when the nurse reached for him.

"Hey, come on, he'll be good," I whispered against her sweaty brow. "They need to check him out."

"He looks fine," she protested.

She was right, he did. He was small, but still six pounds dead on the nail, so was a good weight. He really was a strong little guy and pretty impatient if his early arrival was anything to go by.

"I know, but we need to check those lungs." The nurse smiled softly and held her arms out to take the baby. "You decided on a name, or shall I write Baby Maples for now."

We'd discussed names and while we couldn't fully agree there'd been one that we kept coming back to. I looked to Bronte and decided she could make the final decision—she damn well deserved the honor.

"Everett Carter Maples," she replied, looking down and stroking his head. "Rett for short."

I breathed in shakily. I thought we'd agreed on Joseph as a middle name for a boy, but I'd been wrong.

"Hey, Rett," I whispered and brushed a kiss on his downy blond hair.

"You know Everett means strong, right?" Annalise said as Bronte finally handed over the baby to the nurse. "I think you chose well."

"Yes, I think we have," Bronte replied, her gaze intent on the nurse taking the baby away.

"Okay," Dr. Baskin came up next to me and scribbled something on a chart before looking up. "No stitches, Bronte, so that's good."

"What about Everett?" she asked. "Is he going to be okay?"

The doctor grinned. "Great name. My great grandpa was Everett. He was a good man."

Bronte and I looked blankly at him, having no interest in his family tree, we were more interested in our own.

"Sorry," he said. "You want to know about your son. The good news is his lungs seem okay—"

Bronte shuddered out a, "Thank God." But Dr. Baskin held up his hand.

"We don't know for sure, until we do the tests. All I'm saying is on quick examination they seem fine. He screamed pretty good too."

I smiled as I had to agree with him. He screamed blue murder, only stopping once he was skin on skin with Bronte. As Everett snuggled against her, Dr. Baskin had a quick listen to his chest and because he was happy with what he heard, we'd been given a little more time with him than we'd expected to have. Enough time for him to latch on to Bronte and feed for a couple of minutes. I thought I'd seen a lot of beautiful things in my job but watching the love of my life feed my son had to top everything.

"Right," the doc said. "I'll leave you to get some rest and let your families know the good news."

I held out my hand and when he took it, I shook it hard. I couldn't thank him enough, even if he was too damn handsome to have been hanging around Bronte's pussy as often as he had.

"Thanks, Dr. Baskin," I said, taking in a breath. "Thank you. So much."

"No problem. I'll pop in and see you before I leave, but rest assured Everett is in good hands." He pointed at me. "In fact, I do believe your sister works in pediatrics, right?"

"Yeah," I replied, actually feeling an unusual swell of pride for Ellie. "She does."

"So, you know how great the staff here are."

"Will Rett go onto Ellie's ward?" Bronte asked, reaching for my hand.

"Probably NICU for a short time, while we do the tests and make sure he's all good. Then after that possibly." He smiled at us both. "Or even home. Now, go tell that huge gang of people in the visitor's room that they have a little boy joining the family."

A few minutes after he'd left, Annalise made her excuses too. She'd been amazing in helping to keep Bronte calm and I made a mental note to buy her the biggest bouquet of flowers I could find. We thanked her, Bronte cried, Annalise cried, they hugged and then it was just us two left in the dimly lit room, with the rising sun peeking under the blind at the window.

"I hate he's not with us," Bronte whispered as she brushed a tear from her cheek. "He might be scared. Do you think he thinks we've given him away?"

I chuckled softly. "No, baby, I don't. He knows we love him."

The door opened and a nurse came into the room carrying a blanket and two takeaway mugs.

"Something to drink and for you." She nodded at the blanket. "In case you want to stay with Bronte until you can go and see the baby."

"We can see him soon?" I asked, clutching Bronte's hand.

The nurse grinned. "Sure can, honey. Once Bronte's had some sleep and maybe a little bite to eat then we'll take you to see him."

She deposited the blanket on the end of the bed, the drinks on a side table and then left as quietly as she'd come in.

"You should go and see everyone," Bronte said around a loud yawn. "Show the pictures you took. But not that one of me, I look awful."

"You look beautiful," I replied, kissing her eyes as they fluttered closed. "Get some sleep and I'll be back in a few."

She nodded and snuggled down under the blanket. I was pretty sure she was asleep before I'd even reached the door.

"Oh my God, he's here," Mom cried as I walked into the visitor's room. "Tell us, is everything okay?"

Everyone gathered around me, but Mom and Darcy pushed them all out of the way to get closest to me. When I pulled my phone from my pants' pocket Darcy shrieked like a teenage girl.

"You have a picture. Oh, my goodness."

"Okay, honey," Jim said, pulling her back against his chest. "Let Carter tell us all about it first."

She grumbled under her breath at him, but I knew she meant nothing by it. They were back on track. Jim had been home a month and it had meant everything to Bronte that all was good between them again.

"Do I have a niece or nephew?" Ellie asked, leaning tiredly against Hunter.

"Please let it be a nephew." Austen's voice rumbled from behind her and I was surprised he was there, seeing as he no longer had to have a sitter and had been home alone. "It's bad enough Mom insisted Dad come fetch me when I could have been sleeping, so please God I hope it's not another girl to really top my night off."

So, that explained that. I laughed and took a breath, looking at all the expectant faces staring at me.

"We have a son," I rushed out. "He's beautiful. A little tuft of blond hair, my eyes, Bronte's mouth and nose and—"

"Does he have your winky, honey?" Mom asked in all seriousness. "Because I gotta say, you may have been covered in poop but your winky and cahoonas were pretty impressive for a newborn. Weren't they, Henry?"

"Sure were. You were a Maples through and through."

"I still am," I protested. "And yes, my boy is packing, okay?"

Mom slapped my back. "I knew he would be. Anyway, less penis talk, we want a name and a picture."

I rolled my eyes—she'd been the one who started the conversation.

"Yes, c'mon, buddy," Hunter added. "What've you named him?"

"Baby," Ellie cooed to him. "I've told you. It won't be Hunter."

She rubbed his chest as he pouted and I kind of wished I'd just stayed in the room with Bronte.

"Just tell them the name, Carter," Austen groaned. "Then I can go home and back to bed."

"Okay, he's a strong little guy and we didn't know when we both said we liked it, but this name means strong and fierce. I let Bronte pi—"

"Dude, really." Austen sighed and slapped his forehead. "Just tell us, show us a picture and then go back to my sister."

God, he was getting to be a little turd.

I pulled up the picture on my phone—my favorite. It was one Annalise took of the three of us. Bronte and I were gazing down at our son, while he looked right at the camera; already loving the limelight.

"This is my son, Everett Carter Maples. Weighing six pounds exactly and he came out screaming from what we hope are a good set of lungs."

Everyone cooed and gushed how gorgeous he was, and I'd never felt prouder. I got slaps on the back and hugs and I knew that deep-down he was going to be okay. My son was perfect and even though he was early, he was a fighter and we would all be home together before long.

"Hey," Hunt said. "Something I need to ask."

I turned to him with a smile, thinking he was going to ask if he'd be Godfather. "Yeah, what is it?"

"Did he shit himself like his dad?"

I have no idea why everyone thought he was so damn funny—I thought he was a dick and no, he was not being Godfather.

CHAPTER 31

Bronte

I t was time. We were going home with our baby.

Nine days after giving birth, it was finally the day that we started the new chapter in our life. Everything had been great with Rett's lungs and all the other tests came up negative too. Which was why when his weight and temperature dropped overnight, the NICU doctors wanted to keep him in. For three days Rett's weight dropped each day and I had never been so scared in my whole life.

Carter was amazing. So strong and dependable. If I'd ever worried about his ability to be a parent or whether he was committed, he'd certainly proved me wrong over the last nine days. He'd held me, he'd soothed me, and he'd listened to everything the medical team told us when I was too much of a wreck to take it in. He was a total rock.

Finally, Rett's temperature went up and his weight climbed over the next four days, stabilizing enough for us to take him home.

"You got everything?" Carter asked, making one last sweeping look of the room that my dad had paid for me to stay in so we could be near to our baby.

"Yep," I replied, feeling a buzz of excitement rushing through my veins. "All set."

Carter grinned at me, his eyes shining with anticipation as he then turned to Rett in his baby carrier.

"Hey, little dude. We're going home now." Softly dropping a kiss to Rett's head, I heard him draw in a shaky breath.

"You okay, baby?" I asked, rubbing a hand down his back.

He looked at me over his shoulder and let go of the air he'd inhaled. "Yeah, just can't believe we finally get to take him home."

Both our gazes strayed to Rett and just as we'd done for many minutes and hours over the last nine days, we simply stared and marveled that he was ours.

"We are so lucky, Carter." I swallowed the lump forming in my throat. "Things could have been so much worse."

His hand came to rest on top of mine on his shoulder, and he gave my fingers a squeeze.

"Yeah, I know. They weren't though and now it's time to go home." He checked the straps, for the fourth time and then picked it up, holding out his other hand to me. "Okay, Lollipop, let's go home."

*

"What the fu-flip are they doing here?" Carter groaned as we pulled into the parking lot of the apartment block.

I could see at least four vehicles that I recognized. It appeared that pretty much the whole of our combined family had turned up to welcome us home.

"I told Mom we'd call when we were settled." He turned the engine off and slammed the truck into park. "Stay here, I'll go get rid of them."

As he moved to get out, I pulled on his arm. "Baby, it's fine. They're excited is all."

They hadn't seen Rett apart from in pictures, so it was no wonder they'd all turned up to welcome us home.

"I wanted to get you alone." Carter pouted and looked up toward the window of our apartment.

"You do know I'm not really able to have sex yet, right?" I winced at the thought of him even pointing his mammoth penis in the direction of my vagina.

"What do you take me for?" He turned on me, looking totally pissed.

"I could maybe manage a blowie, or a hand job," I offered.

A huge smile broke out on his handsome face. "You think?"

I slapped his arm. "No, I don't." Narrowing my eyes on him, I then leaned forward and kissed his cheek. "Maybe tomorrow, baby."

He sat up like a little puppy and practically wagged his tail. "You *really* think?"

Rolling my eyes, I unbuckled my seatbelt and looked into the back where Rett was fast asleep. The love in my heart for him was immense. I felt like I had a balloon inside it that was getting bigger and bigger, pushing it out of my ribcage and forcing the air from my lungs.

"You ready for the rest of our lives?" Carter asked, leaning in close to me and watching our son too.

"Yes, I most definitely am."

He pulled me into his side and kissed my temple, breathing me in and I knew I would never want to ever be anywhere else, other than with this man.

"We're going to be awesome, Lollipop, you know that, right? The best parents on the fucking planet."

"Carter," I scolded, nodding toward our sleeping baby. Right at that moment, Rett let out a huge fart, followed with a noise that pretty much told me he'd filled his diaper.

"What the hell has that kid been eating?" Carter cried, holding his nose.

"Just milk."

Carter's eyes came directly to my tits and he licked his lips.

"No," I snapped, but with a little twitch to my lips. "Don't even think about them."

"Not even a little?" he asked, frowning and holding his thumb and forefinger inches apart.

I shook my head. "Nope."

He tilted his head on one side and narrowed his eyes as he thought about what I'd said.

"Okay, Lollipop, consider this," he said and then paused to look at Rett. "Damn, son, that shit stinks." He then turned back to me. "As I was saying. Consider this, I take a picture of your tits and then I can use that to look at and obviously think about that rather than the real thing. How does that sound?"

I just couldn't look at him, because no matter how infuriating he was, he made me want to laugh so much. As I pretended to consider his proposition, Rett let out a huge scream, a hungry scream. I'd already learned his cries in the nine days he'd had my heart—his tired one started off as a grizzle and built up to a crescendo, while his hungry one was a straight-out scream.

"He's hungry." I grinned at Carter. "Sorry baby but looks like he gets first dibs on the tits."

Carter's mouth dropped open and his head swiveled to Rett, who was in full flow.

"Son, we're going to have to have words," he said, reaching over to unclip the baby from his carrier. "We both have a thing for Momma's titties, and they were mine first. However," he said, cradling him in his arms. "You need them much more than I do at the moment, so I'm going to loan them to you. Remember, though, when you get a little older and maybe get some teeth, well they're mine again and mine alone. We got that?"

It was probably gas but Rett actually looked at his daddy and smiled. His eyes seemed to be following Carter's lips as though he fully understood what he was saying. Then he let out another huge fart.

"Okay," Carter said with a chuckle. "I think we have that cleared up." He looked up at me and smiled. "Ready to meet the crazy crowd?"

Feeling like the sun was beaming down on me and warming me from the tips of my toes to the top of my head, I reached my arms around both of my boys.

"I love you so much, Carter Maples," I sighed resting my brow against his. "I don't think there's a man on this planet who I'd rather have as my baby daddy. You're right, we've got this and we're going to be awesome parents."

Carter's hand came to cup my cheek and he let out a soft breath. His eyes searched my face as his fingers gently caressed my skin.

"I love you more than you will ever, ever know," he said softly. "We are going to rock the rest of our lives and this kid is going to be glad he was born our son. Now, about that picture of your titties."

EPILOGUE

Jefferson

Watching my son and seeing the way he looked at his girl, reminded me of how I was with his mom. Sondra had been the love of my life and when she went, I'd never felt pain like it. We were supposed to grow old together, watch Hunter settle down and have kids of his own but I guess that wasn't the greater plan for her. I found it hard to say it was God's plan because I wasn't sure I believed in a god any longer. If there was one, why the fuck would he let someone as sweet and beautiful as my wife be taken from me and Hunt.

Okay, so years had passed, and I was finally moving on with my life, but it didn't mean I'd ever forget her. She'd always be with me and I was pretty sure that was why I'd never met anyone else I wanted to settle down with. I'd played around a hella lot in the last couple of years because let's face it, there's only so long a man can go without fucking. I thought I'd done well going without for four years before I'd got back on the horse. That was how much I loved Sondra. Any sooner and it would have felt like I was cheating on her.

Recently though the 'no strings sex' of the last few years had got a little tiring and it had to have been at least six months since I'd done anything except use my hand.

"So, Pop," Hunter said, as Ellie moved off his knee. "You sure you don't mind the wedding planner and Ellie's folks coming here?"

I waved him away. "Nah, it's fine. Although why Melinda would want to do a kitchen remodel, I have no idea. Nothing wrong with the kitchen she had, if you ask me."

Ellie laughed as she picked up our coffee cups to leave the den and take them into the kitchen. "You sound just like Dad. He's done nothing but complain about how much it's costing him in both the remodel and dinner out as Mom has no place to cook."

"You see why I let Ellie pick the kitchen in the first place," Hunter said with a grin. "Now, I know I won't have to remodel it because it was her choice."

Ellie smiled a little secretive smile to herself. She knew what I knew— she was a woman and would be bored with that kitchen before their first kid had reached Elementary school.

"What time will she be here anyway?" I asked, strangely feeling a little anxious about the meeting and no idea why. It wasn't like she was coming to see me.

"Any time now," Ellie called from the doorway. "She's moving here from L.A., so she's been in town finalizing her house purchase."

"Moving here, from L.A.? Woah that's one hell of an uproot." I shook my head wondering why anyone would choose Dayton Valley out of all the towns in the state. I loved the place, but it was my hometown and L.A. it was not.

"Apparently, she's from around here originally," Hunter said. "Katherine Hallahan, you know her?"

"Nope." I shook my head. "Doesn't ring a bell."

"Yeah, and I reckon you know most of the ladies from around and about."

I rolled my eyes but couldn't stop the grin. He was right, I'd had a great time with the ladies.

"Anyone home?"

Melinda pushed through the door flicking her long, glossy dark hair over her shoulder. Henry followed behind carrying a huge casserole dish with a plate of muffins and cookies balanced on top.

"Honey, you could have carried the sweet stuff at least," he complained. "Hey guys. Hunter, will you take the plate before it falls?"

Hunter took it with one hand and the casserole dish with his other. "I'll take them through to the kitchen."

"The casserole is for you guys and the cake and cookies for when the Wedding Planner gets here. It's all from Darcy," Melinda offered before dropping onto the couch next to me and kissing my cheek. "You ready for this, big guy, our kids getting hitched?"

"Can't say I am," Henry interjected. "She's my baby and no disrespect, buddy, but he's *your* son."

"Hey, I hear ya," I replied. "But Hunter isn't me and I'm not really the me you've seen the last couple of years. You know that."

Henry snorted. "Like you weren't a dog during high school."

"Yeah, I heard all about you and Tracee Wickerson." Melinda raised her brows. "Does our local pig farmer know you banged his daughter under the bleachers?"

"No," I cried. "And he doesn't need to. The point is that once I met Sondra, I was done. I loved her and no way would I have done anything to hurt her."

Melinda took in a deep breath and rubbed my arm. Sondra's death had hit her hard too. They, with Darcy, were best friends, but even before Darcy started to date Jim, Melinda and Sondra were real tight.

"Okay," Henry said lightly, breaking the sadness threatening to smother the room. "I vote we quickly do shots before she gets here. The alcohol running through my veins might lighten the damn load of cash she's going to tell me I'm going to have to hand over."

"Hey," I said, pushing up from the sofa. "I told you, we're going half and half. He's my son, half those guests will be our friends and family."

"Whatever, buddy. We'll sort something out."

"Okay," I said. "I'll go get us some drinks."

Before I had a chance, I heard the sound of car wheels on the gravel outside. It sounded like our wedding planner had arrived. The way her tires screeched I guessed she thought she was running late.

"Ellie, Hunter, your lady is here," I called.

Within seconds, giggling like two little kids, they came bundling into the room.

"Oh my God," Ellie gushed. "I'm so nervous. What if I hate everything she suggests?"

Hunter stood behind her and massaged her shoulders. "You're the client. She has to do what you want."

"I guess so," she breathed out.

"I'll go let her in." Henry said, as he was closest to the door into the hallway which led to the front of the house.

The rest of us stood around, looking at each other, all anxious as if we were meeting the Queen of England, not a wedding planner.

I heard the door open and Henry say hello, followed by the click of heels on the tiles and a sexy rasp of a voice. Whoever she was, she sounded like she ought to be singing in some smoky jazz club.

"So sorry, the damn traffic was an absolute bitch and I thought I was going to be late. I had to give some guy in a brown truck a little encouragement, he was driving so damn slow through the center of town. Oh, hang on can you give me a second, I need to run back to my car for something." All of it was said in what seemed like one breath, without any response from Henry who entered the room and stared at us, wide-eyed.

"What?" Melinda hissed.

Henry's brows arched and he waved his hands around which I think meant boobs and curves.

"She's real familiar too."

"You think you've seen her in a porn movie?" Melinda asked in all seriousness.

"Mom." Ellie groaned. "She's a wedding planner, not a porn star."

"But dad says she has curves," Melinda protested.

"Doesn't mean she's been in a porn movie," Ellie whispered as we heard heels clicking again.

"I don't think so, honey," Henry said, frowning. "I'd have remembered her. Although, it could be the one we watched last week with the woman who masturbated every time she saw a fire fighter."

"Oh god," Ellie groaned. "Kill me now."

"It was quite a good story, actually," Melinda replied. "Not all porn is bad, sweetheart."

"Guys," I warned and cleared my throat as the door into the den pushed open.

A woman with long, lustrous hair in about three shades of brown, stepped inside and I almost fell backward. Henry was right, she had fucking curves to die for. She was a walking, talking hourglass. Her boobs were big, and a fucking amazing cleavage peeked above the V-neck of the tight red jersey dress she was wearing. Her hips flared out from a slim waist, but she had a small curve to her stomach that showed me she wasn't one of those women who just ate salad. And, when my eyes travelled down to her legs, I had to swallow back a groan of appreciation. They were long and tanned and on her feet were the highest pair of black shoes I'd ever seen.

"Well, well, well," she said in her hot as fuck voice. "It is you."

I looked up, finally taking note of the plump red lips, smoky eyes, a perfect little upturned nose and the beauty spot on her right cheek. I thought my eyes were going to pop out of my head as it suddenly hit me who was standing in my den looking like my wildest wet dream ever.

"*Kitty?*" I asked, taking a step closer to get a better look. "Kitty Carmichael?"

"Norm's niece," Henry cried. "Kitty from high school." He pointed at me and then back to Kitty. "You two… shit."

I felt my cheeks heat up, but to her credit Kitty appeared as cool as a winter frost. She had been my first real girlfriend, and when she and her family moved to Florida, when we were fifteen, I'd been heartbroken for about a month; then Sarah Beckett offered me a blow job at my sixteenth birthday party, so…

The reason my cheeks were burning though was because Kitty had been the girl that I'd lost my cherry to. She'd been hot then with quite a rack for a fifteen-year-old but now she was fucking spectacular. If I recalled correctly, and I knew I damn well did, even then, after our first pretty sketchy attempt at sex the other couple of times before she left town had been awesome. For two fifteen-year-old kids we had one helluv an idea of what to do.

"I guess you're thinking what I'm thinking," Kitty said, leaning closer to me. "And yeah, you're right, I am even better now."

Pre Order The Beef Game, coming in the Summer 2021.

THE JACKPOT SCREWER PLAYLIST ON SPOTIFY

shorturl.at/lACL9

Tender	-	Blur
Party in The USA	-	Miley Cirus
Juice	-	Lizzo
I Hope You're Happy	-	Blue October
Watermelon Sugar	-	Harry Styles
My Girl Lollipop	-	Bad Manners
Power Over Me	-	Dermot Kennedy
The Impossible Dream	-	Carter The Unstoppable Sex Machine
Count on Me	-	Bruno Mars
When Doves Cry	-	Prince
Ten Storey Love Song	-	The Stone Roses
Adore You	-	Harry Styles

NIKKI'S LINKS

If you'd like to know more about me or my books,
then all my links are listed below.

Website:
www.nikkiashtonbooks.co.uk

Instagram
www.instagram.com/nikkiashtonauthor

Facebook
www.facebook.com/nikki.ashton.982
Ashton's Amorous Angels Facebook Group
www.facebook.com/groups/1039480929500429

Amazon
viewAuthor.at/NAPage

Audio Books
preview.tinyurl.com/NikkiAshtonAudio

nikki ashton

Printed in Great Britain
by Amazon